BRICK DUST AND BONES

BRICK DUST AND BONES

M.R. FOURNET

FEIWEL AND FRIENDS
NEW YORK

A Feiwel and Friends Book
An imprint of Macmillan Publishing Group, LLC
120 Broadway, New York, NY 10271 • mackids.com

Our books may be purchased in bulk for promotional, educational, or
business use. Please contact your local bookseller or the Macmillan
Corporate and Premium Sales Department at (800) 221-7945 ext. 5442
or by email at MacmillanSpecialMarkets@macmillan.com.

Library of Congress Cataloging-in-Publication Data

Names: Fournet, M. R., author.
Title: Brick dust and bones / M. R. Fournet.
Description: First edition. | New York : Feiwel and Friends, 2023. |
  Audience: Ages 9–12 | Audience: Grades 4–6 | Summary: Twelve-year-old
  Marius Grey has a job as a Cemetery Boy, looking after the ghosts in his
  family's graveyard, but he also hunts monsters and, along with his
  flesh-eating mermaid friend, must race against the clock to save the
  ghost of his dead mother.
Identifiers: LCCN 2022046330 (print) | LCCN 2022046331 (ebook) |
  ISBN 9781250876027 (hardback) | ISBN 9781250876034 (ebook)
Subjects: CYAC: Supernatural—Fiction. | Ghosts—Fiction. |
  Monsters—Fiction. | Cemeteries—Fiction. | Mothers and sons—Fiction. |
  LCGFT: Paranormal fiction. | Monster fiction. | Novels.
Classification: LCC PZ7.1.F6786 Br 2023 (print) | LCC PZ7.1.F6786 (ebook) |
  DDC [Fic]—dc23
LC record available at https://lccn.loc.gov/2022046330
LC ebook record available at https://lccn.loc.gov/2022046331

First edition, 2023
Book design by L. Whitt
Feiwel and Friends logo designed by Filomena Tuosto
Printed in the United States of America by Lakeside Book Company,
Harrisonburg, Virginia

ISBN 978-1-250-87602-7 (hardcover)
1 3 5 7 9 10 8 6 4 2

DEDICATED, IN LOVING MEMORY,
TO UNCLE RAY AND AUNT MARGIE

CHAPTER ONE

$\int$omeone once asked Marius Grey what he thought dread tasted like, and he said, with complete confidence, that it tasted like a penny.

The atmosphere fires electric when a monster enters a room. Those hairs standing on end, that sense of foreboding—it all begins with a spark. Copper and metal fried with a charge. Only terribly boring people manage to ignore a thing like that.

"You know, monsters just prefer to torment houses with terrible electricians. Any room smells of metal if wires are laid bare. It's not supernatural."

Marius tasted a mouthful of pennies while crouching inside Violet Humphrey's closet. He could see her through the slats in the shuttered doors leading to her room. Her mother had dutifully shut them without knowing he was hiding behind the rack of dresses and stuffed animals. It had taken great effort to slowly pry them apart and watch over the girl.

"I have it on good authority that most electricians in Orleans Parish are drunks and gamblers. That is why there are so many hauntings."

"Enough, Mom," Marius whispered in the dark. "Like with most things, you are only seventy-five percent right. What about monsters in the wild? No electricity."

"They are exceptions, but you shouldn't talk back to me. It's rude."

There were several unusual things about this particular whispered conversation in an unsuspecting child's closet. One was that Marius Grey was talking to a disembodied voice. He sat alone with only his book to keep him company. Another was that the disembodied voice belonged to his mother, who was, by all accounts, deceased.

"Leave me alone. I have to watch the girl," he snapped.

Violet, age seven, slept fitfully with her dirty-dishwater hair sprayed around her pillow. She seemed subconsciously aware of the danger building in the real world as she squeaked and thrashed in her sleep. Marius held his breath, waiting for it to appear. Monsters were patient but only to a point. It should not be long now.

He slowly shifted his weight inside the closet. His left leg was nearly asleep. Moving his body let the blood flow back into it, and pins and needles came along for the ride. It took biting down on his lip to hold in his groans of pain, but hey, whatever worked, right? He would not have little

2

Violet Humphrey fight this battle alone. What kind of monster hunter would that make him?

As if bidden by his thoughts, black tendrils reached out from beneath Violet's bed. One at first, and then two and three and seven. If you did not know any better, you might think a great inky octopus was emerging from some dark coral home. He wished it were an octopus. Violet probably wished the same thing.

The boogeyman's body solidified, revealing a long coat made of wispy shadows and a top hat of fine velvet. He breathed in and out, solidifying his form. He stretched bony hands and cracked knobby fingers. Marius spotted a pointed nose and ghoulish grin. His hat was pulled down over his eyes, but every good hunter knew what lay beneath.

"Violet," the boogeyman hissed in the quiet evening. "Violet Humphrey, awaken and look upon me."

The mop of hair stirred until she lay right side up. Her petite nose flared naked in the moonlight. She took in a few tentative sniffs and stiffened. A tiny squeak of fear turned into a hiccup in her throat as she rolled over to face the boogeyman. The poor thing clutched her blanket to her chin despite the warm night.

"Look into my eyes, Violet," the boogeyman said. "Look here, child."

"No," she said, sitting up. Her wide eyes peeked out from beneath the curtain of hair in her face. "No, I won't.

I told my baba about you, and she said not to do what you say."

"You will look, child. How can you not?"

"No way," Violet said with a quivering voice. She refused to turn away from the boogeyman, but she shut her eyes tightly in protest.

"Hang on, wee one," Marius whispered. "Almost ready."

Marius leaned forward, allowing room for his book to slip from his impossibly deep inner pocket and into his hand. The volume felt heavy and reassuring. There was nothing like a good, heavy book to make one feel safer. He searched the pages in the dark until he found the ribbon holding the right spot. There it was—the next blank page.

Standing inside the closet was not the easiest thing. Apparently, Violet loved packing the thing full of toys. Marius's foot slipped over a ball that would have upended his balance if he had not caught himself by grabbing ahold of a raincoat on its hanger. Luckily, the boogeyman did not hear. He was too busy beginning his wail.

The scream is horrendous, yet parents do not hear it. It was a blessing and a curse if you were like Marius, a monster hunter at the age of twelve. To hear a shriek so hideous was awful, but it was necessary.

It was like a warning siren. The cocking of a gun before pulling the trigger. If Marius was unable to hear the boogeyman's wail, he might miss his chance. It would put poor Violet in more peril than she already was. When he checked

4

through the slats again, Violet had both hands over her eyes and was weeping.

Holding the book in his left hand, Marius checked his front pocket, the one closest to his heart, for the brick dust he knew was there. He grabbed a heavy helping with his right hand. With a hard kick, the closet door flew open, and Marius emerged, ready to do battle.

The boogeyman turned to him with a sharp snap of his head. His eyes glowed red just beneath the black velvet hat like two demonic headlights on a dark country road. No longer did he shriek. After lighting on Marius, the monster growled the way only beasts do.

"Marius Grey!" the boogeyman said, pointing a long, sharpened finger in his direction.

His terrible jaws opened far larger than any human's mouth could. They created a gash of a smile, like someone had carved it into a blackened tree and then pried it open with a crowbar. When the maw fully opened, there was no holding back the smell of rot and ruin that came from within. The scent of the putrid remains of the children's souls he had devoured.

Violet's eyes were open now, and she looked from the hunter to the boogeyman and back again. The boogeyman ignored her. He was far too preoccupied with the intruder, which was what Marius wanted.

The boogeyman lunged for the hunter, but Marius jumped aside, throwing brick dust into his glowing eyes. The

5

monster threw his head back and shrieked, desperately clawing at his face. Marius ran to Violet's bed and reached for her. She jumped into his arms without hesitation.

"Who are you?" she asked with a squeak in her throat.

"Marius Grey, monster hunter. Here, hold this and don't lose my spot."

Marius handed her the book and put her tiny finger in the page to mark it. The great red volume looked so huge in her arms, but she nodded to him with determination in her eyes. He reached in another pocket for the silver flask of salt.

"I'm going to make a circle with this," Marius said. The boogeyman was still flailing around, trying to get the brick dust out of his face. It was only a matter of time before he succeeded. "When I do, stay in the circle. Whatever you do, stay inside and don't look into his eyes."

He drew a crude salt circle on the floor around Violet and himself. It was just in the nick of time, because the horrid boogeyman rushed toward them, eyes glowing and teeth bared. When he reached the salt, he slammed into an invisible barrier. It was like watching a ghoulish train hit a brick wall.

The creature crumpled to the floor but rose again undaunted. After all, boogeymen are more or less made of mist and fear. There was little time left. If he got the idea to flee out the window, Marius would lose him again for sure. That would mean two weeks of tracking up in smoke.

Marius grabbed the book out of Violet's hands, opened it quickly, and held the blank page toward the boogeyman. As soon as the monster saw the name written on the page, he shrank away, looking desperately for an escape.

"It's far too late for that. I've got you," Marius said.

"So says you, monster hunter! Your puny spells don't . . ."

"Grab the arm, grab the crook. Stomp the ground until it's shook. Invisible line, invisible hook. Get the monster inside this book!"

As he finished the spell, the boogeyman wailed. Marius's book glowed crimson as it sucked the creature inside. All monsters fought the pull, but it was no use. You might as well fight the surge of time or the rise of the sun. The boogeyman's wispy tendrils reached out to wrap around the railings of Violet's bed, but they found no purchase. The book sucked every inch of him inside, and Marius shut the cover soundly on top of him.

CHAPTER TWO

The frightened girl still sat in the circle of salt, trembling all over. She was a tiny thing swallowed up in her large nightgown. All skin and bones underneath a purple tent. Violet wrapped her arms around her knees and breathed in shallow, halting breaths. Marius peeked through the tangle of hair and saw her eyes were closed tightly.

"You can open your eyes now," he said, taking Violet's hand. "He's gone now. You are safe."

Violet's eyes flew open in alarm. She took in her room, scanning for the monster. When she saw Marius's book, still glowing slightly from its catch, she backed away a few feet, kicking salt across the wood floor.

"Do you hear that?" she asked.

"Hear what?"

Now that the world was rid of the wailing boogeyman, Violet and Marius heard everything much more clearly. The noise they focused on was the telltale sound of adult footsteps heading their way.

"It's my parents!"

"Quick! Back to your bed," he said.

Violet ran to her bed, throwing her covers back. Marius grabbed a rug shaped like an anime cat and tossed it over the circle of salt. His first instinct was to head back to the closet, but there was no time. It was too far away. He had to make a quick decision lest he be caught.

Marius threw a bit of brick dust on the floor leading to the door. With a running start, he slid across the wood. He was immensely thankful he'd left his shoes in Violet's closet in order to sneak better. Now he wore only socks. By far, the best thing if you wanted to travel fast across polished wood. The dust propelled his body straight for the approaching footsteps. He just hoped he could hit the corner before her parents opened the door.

Much to the hunter's relief, his shoulder bumped into the corner of Violet's room just as her mother flung open the door. Marius shrank against the wall as much as he was able. The wood came within an inch of hitting his nose. He held his breath and focused on trying to make himself smaller.

"Violet, honey, what is going on here? We heard a scuffle," her mother said, sounding both worried and annoyed.

Warm light poured inside from the hallway, creating a rectangle of illumination across the bedroom. Violet's eyes were wide, and she moved them from her mother to Marius and back again. Her tiny mouth hung open in an uncertain O of surprise.

"Were you dancing again in here?" a fatherly voice said.

A man's shadow gestured toward the rug covering the salt. When she shot Marius another glance, he shook his head slowly. He held one finger over his mouth. It was the universal kid signal to lie to your parents.

"I had a bad dream," Violet said finally.

"A dream bad enough to move your rug?" her father asked.

"Um . . . yeah. A really bad one."

"Well, that doesn't make any sense," her mother said.

"My dream didn't make any sense," Violet said with a shrug. "That's why this doesn't make any sense."

"Why did you get up and move the rug?" her mother asked, sounding more annoyed than before. "The truth now."

"I didn't move the rug. My dream must have done it," Violet said.

There was a long pause, in which Marius shifted the still-vibrating book under his trench coat. The light had dimmed to a gentle radiance. Any sight or sound might give him away. Violet shifted her eyes to Marius once again. A small glow flashed in her eyes. The recognition of an idea that could be equal parts bad and good.

"Daddy gave me a Coke before bed!"

The parents' feet shuffled on the other side of the door. They were quiet as the air shifted in the room. Marius had to admit, it was a great trick. Violet was a smart cookie.

When in doubt, throw one of the parents under the bus, and fathers were usually the best targets.

"You let her drink Coke before bed?" Violet's mother asked. Her voice was rigid. Words came out short and sharp as though she was spitting them through clenched teeth. An anger just barely kept in check in front of the child.

"I didn't think it would lead to bad dreams," her father said.

"Tom, for heaven's sake."

"You're right, Laura. I'm sorry," he said in a placating voice. "Violet, no more Cokes three hours before bedtime."

Violet shrank a touch. Marius could tell this was a bit of a blow. She had given it up to save his hide. Well, to save both of them. If her parents caught him, that would be it. They would kick him out, maybe even call the police. Someone would take his book. In the wrong hands, the boogeyman would escape and go back to feasting on children's souls.

"Here," her mother said. "I'll tuck you back in."

Marius's eyes flashed wide, and he shook his head at Violet. If her mother tucked her in, she would surely turn back around and see him hiding behind the door.

"No!" Violet shrieked.

"Why not?"

"I'm . . . fine. Mama, I'm just fine. Ready to go back to sleep. Good night."

"Oh. Okay, I guess. Good night, sweetie," her mother said.

"No more running around the room, Violet. Straight to bed," her father said.

"Cross my heart, hope to die," Violet said with a cross motion over her tiny chest.

Slowly, her mother and father left the room and shut the door. Marius waited until he heard their footsteps receding down the hallway. When the hunter stood up, he stretched his stiff legs. Squatting in place like that was hell on a body. Violet got down from her bed and tiptoed over to him silently.

"That was close," she whispered.

"Thanks for the cover," Marius said.

"Who are you?" she asked again.

"I'm Marius Grey, monster hunter," he repeated, sticking out his hand.

"But you're a kid," she said, taking him in as best she could in the dark.

"You don't have to be a grown-up to do this job."

"Will . . . will he ever come back?" she said, pointing to the book in his arm.

Her wide eyes began to water underneath her wild mop of hair. She was a clever girl, but she was still a little girl who had seen a great monster. Marius opened his arms wide, and she ran into them. He hugged her tightly until her tiny body stopped shivering.

"He's never going to hurt you again. I promise."

CHAPTER THREE

There were several places in the area to cash in the boogeyman. Some were nice and clean. Others existed on the fringes of towns and attracted the worst kind of magical people. The Habada-Chérie was somewhere in the middle.

It sat on a rather busy street in the bayou town of Houma. The building was made of scarlet bricks with four white columns at the corners. Each column had slits on the sides that looked like fake windows. Marius knew they were fake because the Habada-Chérie had no windows. It had no door. Well, not one the outside world could see.

Marius walked up to the front of the building. The words *The Habada-Chérie* were painted roughly on the outside. It looked more like someone's spray-painted graffiti than an actual sign.

The hunt at Violet's house took less time than he expected. It was only ten o'clock, so the streets were busier than he liked. He should have delayed, maybe even gone home first. Cars zoomed past, and somewhere up the street, people laughed about something he could not hear.

The smell of bayou water and fried fish wafted on the air. All the commotion went on around the building, but no one tried to go inside. Not one person asked why there was no door. The building was bespelled to shrug suspicion and curiosity away.

Marius reached for a brick that stuck out more than the rest. He was about to pull, when that familiar voice interrupted him.

"There are better places you can go to cash in that boogeyman."

"I know them," he said.

"They aren't the best of characters inside. There's Marie Laveau's old place, and the hoodoo place in Metairie."

"All places that will ask questions. They will report me."

"I just . . . worry."

"Don't. It's fine. I'll be quick."

Marius pulled the brick door open. It scraped along the cement ground. He took one last peek around the area before he popped inside and shut the door behind him.

The Habada-Chérie did not cater to tourists looking to bring something magical back home. You would not find those generic voodoo dolls or fake spell-casting candles here. There were plenty of shops in the French Quarter for that.

No, this was where the real practitioners came for their

supplies. There were sacred stones and blades inside glass cabinets. Magical roots, herbs, and powders lined the walls in ancient-looking jars. Despite the dilapidated appearance of the wooden shelves, everything was well organized.

The shop smelled of otherness. Frankincense oil and old wood mostly, but there was something else too. It was faint, but when Marius took in a lungful, he could detect it. The scent of a fire burned out. That singed smoke smell after a campfire died.

"You again?"

The question came from a croaky throat. Marius jumped inside his skin as Madame Boudreaux popped up from behind the checkout counter.

She was ancient. At least, she looked ancient. He was not great at telling an adult's age, but even Madame Boudreaux's wrinkles had wrinkles. She stared down at Marius with her one good eye. The other one was milky colored and blind.

"Good evening, Madame Boudreaux," he said with his gotta-be-polite-to-adults voice.

"Nothing good about it," she snapped.

"I'm here to see Papa Harold," he said.

"Of course you are. What did you get this time?" she asked.

The eyebrow over her good eye arched with the faintest hint of interest.

He did not answer at first. Instead, he pulled the book from one of the deep inner pockets of his trench coat. It still hummed a little. The spine of the book emitted a faint glow. The cover was warm against his body.

"A boogeyman."

"Oh, is that all?" she said with a wave of her gnarled hand. "I thought it was something interesting. Still hiding in kids' rooms, I see. Very creepy, boy."

"Just . . . can I see Papa Harold?" Marius said. He was tired, hungry, and impatient. "I need to exchange it so I can go home."

Madame Boudreaux's face twisted into a deeper scowl. She crossed her arms over her chest like a woman contemplating where to smack him first.

"I mean, please," he said quickly. "Please, can I see him?"

She hobbled over to the edge of the counter. For a frightening moment, Marius was afraid she would come around with a wooden spoon or something. The last thing he needed was another knot on his head. Instead, the old crone banged on the corner and hollered down the hall.

"Harold! You have business to attend to!"

They heard a shuffling in the back room. Something hard fell to the ground with a *thud*. After some moving and scraping, a disheveled-looking man walked out with his arms full of books and bags.

Madame Boudreaux was a short woman. Marius was almost taller than she was. When she stood next to Papa Harold, she resembled a hobbit because he stood at a whopping six foot seven.

"I heard you making a mess, Harold. For God's sake, give those to me," she said in a huff. Papa Harold handed his things down to her. "Stay out of my storeroom! I've told you."

"I was cleaning. You can't get to the top," he said in an unusually high voice for a giant.

"I said leave it be! Now get moving. The kid is here to exchange a boogeyman. Get to it so he will leave. Kids make the other customers nervous."

Marius took a moment to look around the store. There were no customers other than himself.

"Don't say anything. You don't want to get turned into a chicken again."

"Yeah, I was coughing up feathers for a month after that," he said.

"What did you say?" Madame Boudreaux asked.

"Nothing," Marius said.

"I thought I heard . . ."

"It doesn't matter," Papa Harold said, interrupting her. "Let us go do business, young Marius. I'm anxious to see what you caught."

CHAPTER FOUR

Marius made his way through the hall, following Papa Harold. As they walked, Marius started to smell the unmistakable scent of gumbo. There was a dark door at the end with the slightest of yellow lights coming from beneath. The intoxicating aroma must have been coming from there.

He fought the urge to go straight to the kitchen and help himself to some gumbo. Stalking a boogeyman left little time to eat. He'd had to slip into Violet's room early and hide for hours. Fool that he was, he did not think to bring snacks.

They reached the back room where Papa Harold did his business. It was spacious enough to fit a medium-sized round table in the middle with two chairs on either side. Each one was soft and overstuffed. Mustard-and-red striped wallpaper lined the walls, which made him dizzy if he stared at it too long.

There was nothing particularly remarkable about the

room, except for the incredibly high ceiling, which had been vaulted to allow for Papa Harold's towering head.

"Sit, Mister Marius," Papa Harold said, gesturing to the chair across from his. "Let me see what you brought."

Marius removed the book from the inner pocket of his coat and plopped it on the table. The volume was large and bound in red leather. Every monster hunter had their own book. One that only they could wield. His still glowed a bit from the energy inside, but there was no mistaking the title etched on top in grand letters.

Marius Grey's Book of Monsters

"Oh, how lovely," Papa Harold said. His eyes lit up. "What did you catch?"

"A boogeyman that was trying to eat a little girl's soul," he said.

"It's a good thing you intervened. Let's see how much this one is worth."

Papa Harold was not an attractive man. He was tall and gangly with a weather-beaten face full of scars. No matter the temperature, he always wore long sleeves to cover the old wounds beneath. His ears hung from his head like two slices of liver, meaty and heavy. His left one had once been pierced, but something had ripped the ring out. It left the earlobe split in two, like a snake's forked tongue.

A person would have to fight in some major battles to earn all of those scars. Even though Marius was intensely curious about the stories behind them, he would never be so rude as to ask.

Papa Harold produced a large scale and set it down with a *clunk* sound. Next, he placed the book on a flat plate in the middle of the scale.

Mystic scales were only meant for weighing monster books. Once a creature was captured, the hunter placed their book on the scale, and it calculated the monster's worth in Mystical credit. Their life force was worth its weight in Mystic coins.

People like Marius and Papa Harold, those who lived with one foot in the magical and one foot out, required both human money and Mystic money. Real money bought your food, clothes, and other necessities. Mystic money got you everything else. Favors, magical ingredients, and certain spells. Bartering and Mystic coins were the only ways to buy those things.

Marius watched his book glow as Papa Harold tended to the scales. On one scale he placed an ordinary copper penny. On the other he put small metal weights. He silently adjusted the weights back and forth until the two scales were even. Then the book flashed one more burst of light before it faded away.

Papa Harold removed a coin that had once been a penny. It was now a coin about the size of a silver dollar. Unlike a regular silver dollar, this coin was actual silver, solid through and through. On the top of it was stamped, in bold print, the number ten.

"That's it? He was only worth ten?" Marius asked.

His heart fell deep into his gut. So much time and energy, and all it got him was ten measly Mystics. He dropped his gaze and felt like crying. *No*, he thought while swallowing hard. *That's what babies do. Hunters do not cry.*

"I'm sorry, young Marius. You know I don't make the rules. It's the High Mystics that set the price. I think boogeyman energy just isn't worth what it once was."

The High Mystics held the final word on all things supernatural, including how much something was worth. A Mystical coin's value came from their books.

He looked at the coin in his hand, deflated. Marius took the book off the scale and flipped to the page where he had trapped the boogeyman. His energy was no longer there, of course. The scales sucked that away. In its place was a horrifyingly inked portrait of him.

There was a short biography beneath this along with his actual name. Apparently, he had been called Allastain. Not all of them had their own names. Marius thought that if the boogeyman was old enough to have a name, he should be worth more than just ten Mystic coins.

Each page was like that, an ongoing account of every monster the hunter ever caught. Their portraits and information forever cataloged for posterity's sake. He stared at

Allastain's portrait, wishing it could tell him why Allastain was worth so little.

Papa Harold reached an arm across the table and patted his hand. The wooden bead bracelets on his wrist clacked when he did. His hand was warm, and it gave Marius comfort.

"Be careful. He's not as nice as you think."

Marius ignored the voice and put the coin in one of his front pockets. He returned the book to the void of his trench coat.

"You don't have to do this, child," Papa Harold said. "You are a cemetery boy. It's a noble profession. The High Mystics protect your people. Don't you get a stipend from them? Your food and such taken care of?"

"Yes, but it's not enough," he said, pushing those tears back again.

"Enough for what? One of these days you have to tell me what you're saving for."

Marius did not elaborate. He did not even open his mouth. Papa Harold was right that he received an allowance from the High Mystics, but it was regular money. Human money. Enough to buy food and clothes. It was not what he needed. He needed Mystic coins, and you only got those from hunting monsters.

Nothing good came from trying to explain himself. What good would it possibly do?

"Well, your reasons are your own," Papa Harold said

after a handful of moments spent in silence. "What about that mermaid I sent you after six months ago? You never came back with her. I bet she would be at least fifty, if not more. I hear whispers of her in the waters around Algiers Point. My spies are always watching."

"I never found her," he said flatly.

Papa Harold observed the boy hunter for a few minutes. Marius pointed his gaze down, trying not to wallow in his own misery. Only ten. That terrible boogeyman was only worth ten.

"Look here," Papa Harold said, tapping a long finger on the table. "Why don't you go help yourself to a bowl of gumbo? Madame Boudreaux made too much, as always. There's a Tupperware bowl for you to take it in."

Marius brightened, sitting up straight. Madame Boudreaux's gumbo was legendary, but she rarely shared with him. Not since the chicken incident.

"Really? Thank you!"

"That's all right. Go before she sees. She's in a mood today. Just bring back the Tupperware next time you come by."

Marius thanked Papa Harold again and rushed out of the back parlor. The bowl of gumbo was empty before he left Houma.

CHAPTER FIVE

Marius stood before the arched metal sign for his cemetery. It belonged to him because it belonged to his family. Generations of his ancestors had lived here as vigilant caretakers. Their small cemetery was near the town of Lafitte, right off Bayou Rigolettes. When his father disappeared and his mother died, the duties of ghost keeping fell to Marius.

Every cemetery has people who care for it. Most are nearly invisible to your average person. There are humans who are paid to mow the lawns and wash the stones. They are important, but it takes a special kind of person to care for the ghosts.

He was born into a family of cemetery people. That is where he got his name. *Grey* was the last name given to boys, and *Stone* was the name given to girls.

"There's no greater calling, Marius, dear. We cemetery people get to live half in and half out. We get the best of both worlds. It's an honor."

"Yeah, you love saying that," Marius said. "Only seventy-five percent accurate again."

"Ninety-five percent accurate."

"Eighty percent, Mom."

"I will concede to eighty-five percent, but only because I have no physical hand with which to smack you."

"Fine. Deal."

There was no need to whisper anymore or hide the fact that he heard her. He was alone for all intents and purposes. No one to listen in and wonder if he was crazy way out here. No one would ask who he was talking to, and the ghosts did not care.

The sign welcoming people to his cemetery was old and a little rusted. The words read *Greystone Cemetery*. It was a big metal arch over a dirt path barely wide enough to fit a car. Not that it mattered. Hardly anyone was entombed in Greystone Cemetery anymore. Everyone moved to bigger burial sites closer to cities and away from the water.

He stopped just outside the sign. There were the same rows of graves as usual. Tombs and mausoleums with rows of rectangular blocks. Cajuns did not bury their dead this close to the water. One hard rain would raise the bodies and send them on their merry way down the river. Everything was aboveground in stoned coffins.

Most ghosts could not leave a cemetery. If they passed and were properly interred, there was little reason to leave.

Their spirits rested in a lovely afterlife retirement until they moved on to their next place.

There were other deathly outcomes. Disturbed graves or violent passings. Malevolent hauntings only came about when the remains were not cared for. This was why cemetery people were so important. Retired ghosts needed tending to.

It was dark, nearly midnight, but he did not need a flashlight. Marius was a cemetery boy, which meant a hazy light appeared to guide him when he was close to any grave. Now the trail leading him to the cemetery proper was glowing green, welcoming Marius home. The thing was, he did not want to go. Something in his belly kept him rooted in place.

"What's wrong? Why don't you want to go home? Sleep in your own bed. You have to be tired after all of that."

"I don't know why. Because you're there, I guess."

"Marius, you know I'm not really there just like I'm not entirely here."

"All the more reason to stay away."

"My beautiful boy, you know I'm always here to talk to."

"Not right now, Mom. Please stop talking."

"Why, for heaven's sake?"

"Because . . . I miss you a little too much right now to talk to you."

Marius took a deep breath and sighed heavily. His mother did not respond. The voice in his head quieted just like he asked. For some reason, it made him sadder. There was a perpetual cold spot around his back. Right where a mom's arms would go in a hug. It never could fully warm like the rest of his body.

Marius's mother had died almost two years ago, leaving him to fend for himself at the ripe old age of ten. His father had disappeared a year before that. All he had of them were three things. His book of monsters, his mother's raven skull necklace, and his father's enchanted coat.

The coat was one of his prized possessions, even though it hung big on him. The bottom fell almost to his ankles. He had to roll up the sleeves so they did not fall over his hands. It might have looked a little silly, but he did not care.

There were six buttoned pockets on the outside of each breast, making the total outer pockets a whopping twelve. Plus, there were two inner pockets that were enchanted to hold much more than was possible. If you were a monster hunter, you could not ask for a better piece of clothing.

His bed was calling to him, but he turned away. The cemetery bordered the shoreline of the bayou. He decided to make his way over to the small dock that sat just thirty yards from the entrance to the graveyard. The dock was old but well made. It only creaked a little under his feet.

There was a stringer of fish tied to the tallest support post. When he brought it up, he found the trout he'd caught still attached and still alive. The fish flipped its tail at Marius, but he managed to remove it from the line and toss it into the rowboat that was tethered to the dock.

The boat was petite, fitted with oars to propel it through the water. It rocked under his weight once he hopped inside. Ages ago, Marius had made big plans to buy an outboard motor for it, but he'd given up on that dream. That sort of thing was reserved for kids who had parents. Now there was too much on his plate.

He shoved off and used one of the oars to move the boat into the middle of the bayou. The insects sang their nighttime songs, and creatures shifted inside the surrounding greenery. In the distance, Marius heard a few fish break the surface of the water with muffled splashes. When his boat was about where it needed to be, he dropped anchor.

The boy hunter kept a short fillet knife in the lowest outside pocket of his trench coat. The dried jasmine was two pockets above that one. He sprinkled some jasmine in a big circle in the water. With the fish in one hand, he stabbed the knife into its belly, killing the fish immediately. Marius cut and sawed until he was able to pull the guts out in one long yank. He tossed the string of entrails right in the middle of the floating circle of jasmine.

Now it was time to wait.

Marius shut his eyes and took in the scent of the bayou. Brackish water, cypress trees, moss, and fish. The gentle current of life that never moved too fast. But he did not have to sit there long, taking in the night. She came within minutes, meaning she must have been waiting for him.

There was the sound of something gently breaking the

water's surface. The smooth displacement of water. When he peeked over the side of the boat, there was Rhiannon. She had a mouthful of trout guts and dried jasmine stuck to her milky hair.

"It's late," the mermaid said simply in between bites.

"I know. It was a long night," he said.

"I was getting worried," she said.

"Why? It's not like your kind sleeps much."

"Still though."

She swallowed her snack, swam closer, and put both hands on the edge of the boat. Her eyes were wide with moonlit wonder. Her hair hung like fine tendrils of silvery moss around her face. She dug her razor-sharp nails into the wood of the boat to steady herself.

"It was a boogeyman," Marius said with a long sigh. "The one I've been tracking. I got it before it got ahold of a little girl."

"That's my monster hunter," she said. When Rhiannon took in his sullen face, she asked, "Why so sad? That's a good thing, right?"

"Yes, it's good. He was only worth ten though."

"That's not a lot," she said.

"I'll never get what I need at this rate, Rhia."

Rhiannon opened her mouth like she was going to say something but shut it when she saw the whole trout by his foot. Marius noticed her sudden focus. Watching the dilation of her pupils was akin to watching a cat stalk a bird. If there was one thing Rhiannon loved more than anything else, it was food.

"Are you going to eat that?" she asked.

"No. I brought it for you," he said, handing her the rest of the fish.

Real mermaids were not like the ones in Disney movies. They did not swim around singing with fish and saving drowning people. More often than not, mermaids were the reasons ships sank and men got devoured.

Mermaids sang beautiful songs, seducing men to their deaths. They were gorgeous beings, part female and part fish, and horribly dangerous. In fact, mermaids were always female, only reproducing when they decided to lay their eggs in the half-eaten body of one of their victims. Their offspring emerged by eating their way out of the corpses they were born into.

Rhiannon had been snared in a fishing net when she was a child. When the fisherman had big dreams to sell her to the New Orleans aquarium, she ate his face and escaped into the Mississippi. As far as he knew, she was the only mermaid in the river. Most of her kind lived in the ocean.

Bobbing on the water's surface, Rhiannon looked like a thirteen-year-old girl treading water. There was no way to tell how old she *really* was because her kind aged differently than humans. To any onlooker, she had the sweet face of a beautiful girl. Her eyes were a sparkling aquamarine, her skin was the color of milk, and she had delicate hands, if you could get over the sharp talons on each finger.

If you were able to look below the water, you would see small iridescent scales lining the skin around her elbows, underarms, and collarbone. The scales got bigger around her chest, making her look less girl and more fish. There was a spiked dorsal fin on her lower back and one bluish-green tail where a human's feet would be.

She was gorgeous until she ate. A mermaid's version of eating was fairly traumatizing to watch. Her first mouth consisted of a pair of girl lips, pretty and roselike, but her second mouth was a horror show. Rhiannon took the trout by the tail and opened her full maw. Her bottom lip lowered, opening a mouth all the way down to her chest. A nest of needle-sharp teeth lined the upper and lower jaws. A serpentlike tongue whipped out, wrapped around the fish, and pulled it into the cage of teeth.

Marius tried not to wince. It always made her embarrassed when he looked disgusted while she ate. Rhiannon closed her mouth, chewing happily. She was back to looking like a girl again, her cheeks full like she had taken a big bite out of a beignet.

"Papa Harold was asking about you again," he said.

Rhiannon stopped chewing and swallowed hard. She gazed over the boat at him, looking a touch sheepish.

"Have you been playing games around Algiers Point?" he asked.

"No," she said. "Why do you say that?"

"Because there's been sightings around Algiers Point. Come on, Rhia. We talked about this. You know that is central to a lot of the magic community. There's been whispers. Papa Harold has spies everywhere," he said.

"I wasn't luring drunks to their death again, if that's what you're implying," Rhiannon said, crossing her arms. She was doing her best to look indignant. "I'm on a strict fish and alligator diet. Sometimes a boar if I can get one close enough to the water."

"Then what were you doing?" he asked.

"Listening to the music," she said, throwing her upper body onto the boat dramatically. "It's so boring in the bayou. I mean, it was more fun when I could lure fishermen to their deaths, but no. You said no more murder."

"Rhia, you can't just . . ."

"Really, I was just listening to the jazz music. I'm telling the truth, Marius. You can hear it coming from the quarter. It's so pretty."

"Just listening?" Marius asked skeptically.

"Well . . ."

"I'm not the only hunter out there. Someone else might come after you. Rhia, spill it."

"I might have been singing along too," she said with a wince.

"Rhia!"

"I know. I know! I didn't mean to, but some people

heard my song. The next thing I knew, there was a group gathered on the bank trying to take my picture."

"Did they get one?" he asked, trying not to panic.

"No way. It was dark, and I dove down before they could see anything."

Marius bent over and rested his face in his hands. He shut his eyes and tried not to scream. It was all too much. Too long of a night, too much work, and not enough payment for his effort. Too much being on his own in a dangerous world. Now he was responsible for a mermaid too. He could barely keep himself fed and alive.

A small, wet hand wrapped around his. With all of her fishiness, you would think her skin would be cold, but it never was. She was always hot. The temperature a human might be if they had a fever.

"I'm sorry, Marius," she said in a tiny voice.

She did appear sorry, as much as a mermaid was able to seem sorry. They were generally a bunch without remorse, but Rhiannon had lived more life among humans than she had with her own kind at this point. Maybe they were wearing off on her.

"It's all right, Rhia," he said.

"So . . . you won't take me to Papa Harold?" she asked.

"Of course not! I would never. We are . . . friends," he said.

Rhiannon blinked several times, looking surprised. She squeezed his hand in hers. He nearly yelped from the pain. Even he forgot how deceptively strong she was sometimes.

"Really, Marius? We are friends?" she asked.

"I always thought we were," he said. For some reason, saying that made his cheeks blush bright scarlet.

It had been half a year since they met. No matter the bounty on her head, Marius just could not bring himself to cash in. She was an orphan, alone like him. A lonely soul. He could have collected her and gotten the money for her monstrous soul. Instead, he hid her away and told Papa Harold the tales of the Mississippi Mermaid were untrue.

A huge smile spread across her face. Thankfully, it was with her human mouth and not the other one. That might have been too much to handle after the day he'd had.

"Yes! Yes, we are friends."

"Good," he said, smiling. "No more talk about me taking you to Papa Harold, and no more singing near the other humans. I can't protect you if you do that."

Rhiannon nodded, still smiling.

"Promise. Double triple promise," she said. She looked from him to the dock next to the cemetery. "Do you want me to push you home?"

"No. I don't want to go home tonight," he said. The long day and late hour made him yawn. "I think I'll just sleep here."

"Is she . . . does she still talk to you?" Rhiannon asked.

"Yeah. She does. Somehow, it's louder when I'm at home," he said.

"Curl up in the bottom of the boat, okay? I'll sing to you."

He took off his coat to use as a blanket and fashioned a bait net into a pillow. He curled up in the bottom of the boat, comfortable in his makeshift bed. The boat rocked slightly as Rhiannon let go. Marius heard her swim underneath. The song she sang came through the wood of the boat, lulling him to rest and let go of the day.

A mermaid's song was meant to be seductive, but that was not its only purpose. Rhiannon had taught him it could heal, it could soothe, and it could tell a story. Marius lay there in the open air of a Louisiana night with a mermaid friend singing a beautiful song. He fell asleep within minutes.

CHAPTER SIX

Marius awoke to a bright sun. Floating in the boat, out in the open, did not provide shade for a slumbering person. By all rights, he should have been awake for hours. The bright southern day should have forced him to wakefulness just after dawn. Judging by the yellow ball high above, it was at least ten o'clock. He jolted up, and the boat rocked beneath him.

"Rhia?" he asked, searching the water around him. "Rhia, are you still here?"

Nothing but the buzzing of insects greeted him. A large dragonfly flittered nearby and landed delicately on the edge of the boat. That was definite proof Rhia had gone. She adored eating dragonflies. They were her favorite treat. She snacked on them like a human chomping on popcorn. The sparkly bug would already be toast if Rhia were near the boat.

A jolt punched him right in the gut. If it was almost ten, that meant he was late for school. Marius groaned and slapped his face.

"Madame Millet is going to kill me!"

Madame Millet's house stood as it always had, tall and sturdy. It was one of the grander homes in the Algiers Point, boasting two stories, five bedrooms, and who knew how many bathrooms. No matter how huge, it always seemed to be busy with people. One thing Marius never could get over was the horrendous yellow paint job.

"Honestly, it's the color of cat vomit. Well, a cat who ate dozens of those yellow marshmallow birds, thinking they were canaries, and then vomited all over the outside of the house. I will never know what Madge was thinking."

Marius snorted, trying to hide his laugh. He felt much the same way but would never in a million years say it to Madame Millet. That would invite a world of hurt through his door.

"She's not family or anything, Marius. If you are looking for a replacement for me . . ."

"I'm not, Mom. I just . . . like her. She treats me like something other than that sad orphan, you know?"

"All right. Fine enough. Just watch after those cats. They will rip you open with those thumbs of theirs."

Speaking of cats, a feral herd of them lounged about the grand porch of the house. All had more toes than necessary. Polydactyl cats. Several had six or seven toes on each paw. Marius knew because he counted while keeping a safe distance. The herd was intolerant of threatening people. Luckily, they tolerated his presence, but only so far.

He made his way up the creaky steps and rang the doorbell. The door flung open, and Marius found himself face-to-face with Mildred Millet, Madame Millet's eldest daughter.

Mildred was just slightly younger than he was. Marius was twelve, and she was eleven for the next three months. A fact the hunter reminded her of regularly since she hated him. Age was a big deal for them, and having months on an adversary went a long way. She scowled at him with her hands balled on the place where hips would probably go someday.

"What do you want, Mary?" Mildred asked sharply.

"You know that's not my name," he said.

"Whatever, *Mary*. That's your name to me. I get to call you anything I want. *Grey* is such a booooooring name. You know that, right?"

"She's a little brat. Always has been. The most annoying baby I ever met."

"And you're being so annooooooying," he countered in the same voice.

"I ought to pop you one right here."

"Mildred, move. I'm not saying it again," he said.

He was beginning to lose his temper. The muscles tightened around his neck and through his shoulders. Marius was exhausted and ready to lash out. Anything to let loose a little. But no. He knew he had to rein it in.

Her mother did not allow her to bully her twin siblings. They were too young for such things. So she had to vent her bullying somewhere. Marius just wished it were not directed at him at the moment.

"I think I might punch you in the mouth. Then you'd have something interesting about your face. I could call you Mary Rouge when your lip swells up."

"Leave me alone, Mildred," he said, gritting his teeth.

Marius counted backward from twenty. This was Madame Millet's daughter, after all. Clocking her would cost him more than the tardiness.

All of the Millets, Mildred included, were dark complected. Her flawless umber face was a stark contrast to his. Cemetery people like Marius often had the neutral color of ambiguous origins. Anyone walking by would have a hard time telling their ancestry if they were able to spot them at all. They rested directly in the middle of the desaturated color wheel. Best for blending into the background. He could just as easily fade into a crowd as he could a row of gravestones.

However, if you put him next to Mildred, he resembled a faded copy of a copy of a boy. Marius's one startling feature was his blue eyes, which he inherited from his father, who had come from the normal world.

Marius always had a smudge of something or other on his cheeks. His clothes were perpetually dirty. His black hair was forever an unkempt mop on top of his head. Mildred's dark hair was always in elaborate braids with ribbons and beads. Her face always scrubbed clean. She never wore anything that would be considered ratty or wrinkled. It was the difference between having a mom and not.

Marius was about to spit a snide remark back to Mildred when he saw her eyeing his raven amulet. It was a real juvenile raven skull encased in sterling silver with a moonstone inlaid on the top. A powerful talisman. Marius never took it off. Mildred coveted the skull, and he knew it.

"Cheer up," Marius said, brushing off her early insults. "Maybe when you grow up, you can get some real jewelry too. Because . . . you know . . . you are only eleven. Need a little bit more maturity."

Mildred's nostrils flared, and she opened her mouth to retaliate. She was winding up for another round of insults, but he cut her off.

"I'm here for class. You know that," Marius said.

"Class started an hour ago. Maman is almost done with her lesson."

"Well, your maman is probably angry that you're missing it right now," he snapped.

Mildred scowled and balled her fists. Marius glared at her. The standoff would have probably lasted longer if Madame Millet had not interrupted them. Her voice carried from within the house.

"Is that Marius? For heaven's sake, Mildred, let him in. I swear, the two of you."

Mildred did not say a word. She merely stepped aside, giving Marius the opening he needed to enter the house.

They walked through the main hall and into the front parlor without so much as an upward glance.

The snotty girl raced ahead of Marius, being sure to enter the classroom before him. He let her. After all, it was not important to him. Let her have her stupid win. He felt tired all the way inside his bones.

Marius took his normal seat in the back, closest to the door. Mildred sat one back from the front. She made a big show of sitting up straight with a pen and paper at the ready. Message received. Mildred Millet was the good one in the class. Madame Millet, on the other hand, was not impressed.

"Stop trying to show off, Mildred," she said with a slight frown. "Your last math test is nothing to be proud of."

The monster hunter did not mean to snicker, but he did. It came out in a loud snort. A ripple of giggling among the other kids radiated away from him.

"And you, young Mister Grey, have nothing to laugh about," Madame Millet said, turning her attention on him. "You're late today and you left early yesterday. That is not behavior becoming of a proper young man. Would you care to explain yourself?"

Marius shrank in his seat. Of course he could not tell her the real reason. He had left early the day before to camp out in the little girl's closet. Today, he was exhausted from staying up late. Madame Millet would have a fit if she knew he was monster hunting.

"Chores," he said at last.

"Chores?"

"Yes, Madame. Chores around the cemetery. I apologize."

She eyed him for a while. It was impossible to tell what was going on behind those eyes of hers. Was it disbelief or pity? Marius was hoping for disbelief. Pity was the absolute worst.

"Very well, then. Let's proceed with class. I expect you to pay attention."

In this world, there are normal people, magical people, and fringe people. Normal people are easy to understand. They are, well, normal. Your everyday bystander who has no knowledge of magic whatsoever. It describes the vast majority of the human race.

Purely magical people are rare and often extremely powerful. Witches, conjurers, sorcerers, and hermits. People who can do magic without herbs and spell books if they want. They prefer to keep to themselves. If you were to run into one, it would be because you made some really poor decisions in your life.

Fringe people are those who walk in between. They live, and sometimes work, in the normal world, but they walk in magical circles. Most practice magic and work magical jobs. They walk that tightrope between the regular world and the paranormal.

Schooling for normal kids is easy. There are thousands of schools with millions of books to teach them about the world. Of course, they never learn the whole story of the world because they do not understand magic. Magical kids learn at home, and are told to stay away from everyone else.

That leaves the fringe kids to figure out a less-traveled path. Magic and technology rarely mix well, so regular school is out. Witches and conjurers are known for banning fringe kids from their homes, so that's a no go. Thankfully, people like Madame Millet create hybrid schools for the children who live in between.

Marius sank down in his chair and scanned the room. Madame Millet's interesting taste in paint colors continued inside.

The classroom resembled a poorly painted dining room more than a school. In fact, part of it was Madame Millet's dining room. Years ago, she'd had the walls between the parlor and the dining room removed so that she could convert the space into a school.

The ceiling of the classroom was painted a muted shade of blue. There was a weird gradient of color on the walls. It went from a deep aqua green near the floor and faded upward to lighter aqua blue on the top.

Even though it was spacious, the room always made Marius feel claustrophobic, like he'd sunk to the bottom of a lake. If the day went particularly long, he felt like he was drowning.

"As I was saying," Madame Millet continued, opening

her textbook on the podium in the front of the classroom, "today we are learning about emergency spells to do at home. It's always good to know when is the proper time to do what spell. Remember what we always say."

"Only call the ambulance if magic can't fix the problem," the class recited in unison.

"That's right. Now, we just went over some basics of magical first aid. Sorry, Marius, I'm not going back over it. You will have to get the notes from someone else."

Marius nodded. He turned to look at the boy to the right of his seat. It was Antoine.

He liked Antoine well enough. Marius didn't find him nearly as tedious as some of the others. Although he was not sure if he considered them real friends outside of class. They rarely saw each other and only talked when they had something good to trade.

Antoine was fourteen and small for his age. Even Marius, with his lanky form, looked older. He was nice enough though. Rarely had a bad thing to say about anyone.

When Marius looked at him, Antoine nodded.

"Did you get it?" Marius asked.

Antoine stiffened all over, and he averted his eyes.

"Yeah, I got it. It wasn't easy, and I'm gonna get in real big trouble if..."

"Don't worry. No one will link it back to you," Marius said.

"Shhhhhh!"

The sound came from the front of the class. At first, Marius thought the voice was Mildred's. When the boys looked up, they saw the angry glare of Shirley Moore. Antoine flashed a rude hand gesture at her, and she turned back around.

Shirley and her siblings always took the three front seats in school. Shirley, Ramona, and Ethan Moore were the children of two professors. Their parents taught at the same college and were constantly competing with each other over everything. Funding, rankings, approval.

Apparently, their rivalry trickled down to their children. The triplets were absolutely obsessed with getting better grades than their siblings.

Just behind Shirley, and in front of Marius, sat Lynna Trudeau and Molly Fakier. Albert Thibodeaux and his brother Trevor always took the seats in front of Antoine. There was a set of new kids to the right of Marius whose names he never bothered learning.

"I will continue if everyone is done," Madame Millet said, sounding irritated.

Madame Millet was a nice woman to a point, but it would be a mistake to push her too far. She was one of the most powerful fringe priestesses in New Orleans.

"Good. When encountering someone possessed, remember it's best to act first and think later. It's a simple spell with an easy recipe. Now then, can anyone list some of the creatures that can possess a human being?"

45

"Ghosts!" Shirley said, thrusting her hand up after the fact.

"Yes, good. Anybody else?"

"Faeries!" Ethan shouted.

"In some cases," Madame Millet said.

"Wendigos!" Ramona added.

"Well, no. Not really. Those are people who have turned into a monster. They are not possessed. Good try though."

Ramona shrank in her seat. Her brother and sister smiled defiantly at her.

A silence fell over the room as Madame Millet searched their faces. She landed on Marius.

"And you, Mister Grey? What other things can possess a person?"

"Demons."

Marius said it so quickly and clearly, even Madame Millet found herself speechless for a minute. Normally, he did not offer answers in class. Marius tried to make as little effort as possible. He would squirm and yawn, pretending not to hear the question. It was what every teacher expected.

So, when the word *demon* flew out of his mouth with ease, the entire room silenced. Everyone knew his story. They knew what happened to his mother.

"That's ... correct. Good job, Mister Grey," Madame Millet said with a smile. "Now, if you find that someone you know has been possessed, there is a spell that will easily rid them of their unwanted passenger. You need salt, brick dust, holy water, oil, and a rosary."

That reminded Marius that he was low on holy water. There were rumors about some muckety-mucks touring the French Quarter. They would definitely be hitting up St. Louis Cathedral, which would significantly distract the clergy. That meant he had a solid window for collecting holy water.

Madame Millet's talking faded into a low buzz in the back of his mind. So much planning. So many lies. It was hard to keep it straight.

The stomping of a heel on wood floor snapped him back to the class at hand. When he looked up, Madame Millet was eyeing him. She flipped open a small spell book with an agitated flick of the wrist.

"The incantation is quite easy to remember," Madame Millet said, continuing the lesson. "Unwanted thing, illegal traveler. Torment and evil is your goal. Not your time, not your vessel. Get thee gone and release this soul."

Marius half-heartedly wrote it down in his notebook, reasonably sure he would never need it. He normally liked spells, but he was so tired. All he could think about was how he could get more Mystic coins. Alas, there was no spell for that.

CHAPTER SEVEN

When the next teacher entered the room, textbook in hand, Marius groaned inwardly. It was Mrs. Pine. That meant today was math day. He hated both Mrs. Pine and math in equal parts.

Mrs. Pine was a normal person. That was why she was Mrs. Pine and not Madame Pine. *Madame* and *Papa* were reserved for the magical and fringe adults.

Mrs. Pine was painfully thin and fragile looking. You would think those things added up to a gentle person, but that was not the case. What meat she had on her bones was taut and inflexible. When she spoke, it was loud, and when she stepped, it sounded like a horse stomping.

The math teacher lashed out often when provoked. Her temper had a hair trigger, and Marius seemed to always be pressing on it. She reminded him of an angry Chihuahua.

"Good morning, class," Mrs. Pine said. She tried for a smile, but it looked more like a grimace. "Today we will be studying algebra. I have placed your new books underneath your desks."

Everyone groaned collectively. Only the triplets seemed excited for the next lesson, popping up with their books eagerly. Marius considered throwing something at the back of their heads.

"Let's open our books to page thirteen," she said, trying to hide the break in her voice. "Algebra may seem strange to you now, but I promise it will make sense eventually."

As Mrs. Pine began her lesson, her voice settled into that drone teachers had when they read something for a long amount of time. Marius tuned her out. After the long night, he felt sleep calling his name.

Marius thought about the boogeyman, and he thought about Rhiannon. He imagined being home and in his boat at that moment. The gentle rocking of the bayou. Rhiannon's sweet singing beneath his head. Peace. Sweet peace.

A loud *crack* woke him up.

Marius shot up in his seat and found himself face-to-face with Mrs. Pine. She held a ruler in one hand. Her eyes glared at him with sharp concentration. Just behind her, he spotted Mildred giggling behind her hands.

"Mister Grey! Are you so disrespectful of me that you fall asleep in my class? Or is it that you think algebra is not worth your precious time?"

"Yes," he answered, rubbing his eyes.

"Yes to what?"

"I don't know. Both of those," he said defiantly. "No one needs algebra. Not us, anyway. Geometry sure, but not this stuff."

Why Marius disliked the woman was something he could not put a finger on. Maybe it was her demeanor. Perhaps it was the fact that she was always picking on him for not paying attention when others did it too. Either way, he found himself winding her up for no reason.

Someone snickered, but he could not tell who. Marius couldn't help but smile a little, and the teacher saw it. Mrs. Pine's face flushed with anger. She smacked his desk with the ruler again. Her breath came hard and ragged.

"You will be respectful, young man!" she shouted.

"Or what?"

Normally, Marius would not antagonize her this much, but he was tired and cranky. He wanted to go home. Maybe if he pushed her enough, he would get sent away.

"You little . . ."

Before Mrs. Pine could spit out her threat, Madame Millet intervened. Apparently, the ruckus was loud enough to bring her running.

"Mrs. Pine, I'd like a word, please. In my office," Madame Millet said sternly.

The math teacher stopped and stood up straight. She looked like someone had stuck a rod in her spine. Mrs. Pine took a few deep breaths and turned to face her employer.

"Yes, Madame."

Mrs. Pine placed her ruler on her desk and followed Madame Millet out of the classroom. Marius let out a sigh of relief, but it was premature.

"And you, young Mister Grey. Go wait out in the hall."

Marius groaned and got up from his desk. Antoine shot him a sympathetic look while Mildred laughed out loud.

"See ya, Mary. Good luck or whatever."

There was a door that stood in between him and Madame Millet's office. It was painted red with symbols etched into it in gold. The words were large and plain as day in a loopy script.

All who come are welcome. All who leave in anger are fools.

The people who sought out Madame Millet's tarot readings and psychic predictions probably thought this was cute. A fun sign to warn them to take her advice or face the consequences. What they did not know was this was an immensely powerful incantation. If you crossed the door and angered her, the door cursed you without you even knowing it.

There was murmuring within. Mrs. Pine and Madame Millet argued on the other side of the door. Well, it sounded more like Mrs. Pine was doing all the shouting and Madame Millet was talking her down.

Marius tiptoed across the hall and pressed his ear to the door.

51

"I can't do this, Madge. This magic thing is too weird. With everything I have to deal with and that impudent Marius boy. It's too much!"

"I need you to calm down. When's the last time you ate something?"

"That's not relevant. Did you know someone threw some powder in my coffee two weeks ago that made me sneeze purple for three days? Before that, there was the incident with the glowing book."

"The what?"

"The one in his pocket."

"Whose pocket?"

"Marius Grey! He's hiding something. Did you hear those snide remarks?"

"He's twelve, Charlotte. Just a lost twelve-year-old boy needing an education."

"He's not just a little boy. None of them are."

"Listen, I can't teach all the things these kids need. I'm no professor. Spells and history, sure. Math and science I need to farm out. The Home School Advocacy referred you highly. I expected you to comport yourself better than this," Madame Millet said evenly.

There was a pause. A long one.

"This is not . . . what I thought it would be. My God, Madge, I'd never heard of such things before I came here. Not outside the movies. Spells and creatures? For heaven's sake, I'm Baptist!"

"Spells and creatures are what we deal with here. That's the world we live in. I pay you good money to teach these children math and science. No one would pay better."

"I could be home taking care of my sick kid, but instead I'm here, and Marius doesn't even have enough respect to stay awake!"

Mrs. Pine's voice was quivering, while Madame Millet sounded calm. She managed to be firm but caring at the same time. It was how she sounded with practically everyone, and it was highly effective.

"But that Marius . . ."

"Is a kid who lost his parents," Madame Millet said.

The conversation went silent for a while. Those words made Marius's heart sink into his stomach. It felt like he was digesting a hunk of lead.

"A kid who lost his parents," he whispered to himself.

Was that how people saw him? The entirety of him wrapped in a bundle and labeled a tragedy.

"Don't listen to that. Madge is just saying those things to get that awful woman to cut you some slack."

"That's not what it sounded like," he whispered to the voice in his head.

Suddenly, a stampede of little feet rounded the corner. Marius looked up to see Mildred's twin siblings giggling and running straight for him. Little Mina and Marcel.

Madame Millet was awfully fond of naming her children with the letter *M*. Her first name was Madge, after all. For the life of him, Marius could not remember her husband's name. A heart attack had taken him a year ago.

The twins danced around him, laughing like crazed sprites. They were not quite three yet. Skinny bodies with plump cheeks. Their voices carried in the quiet hallway.

"Mary, Mary, quite contrary! How does your garden grow!"

"Shush, both of you!" he hissed at them.

"With stonework eggs and spider legs and candles all in a row!"

"Be quiet! Your maman will hear," he said.

It was too late, of course. When he looked up, there were Madame Millet and Mrs. Pine staring down at them. He was caught.

CHAPTER EIGHT

Mina and Marcel squealed in unison and ran away. They started up singing again in that frantic tone of excited children. Their song could be heard echoing through the house.

"Mary, Mary, quite contrary..."

The spindly math teacher eyed Marius. It was not the scornful gaze she'd used earlier, nor was it particularly kind. There was something else in it. Maybe pity? He would have preferred anger over pity any day.

Mrs. Pine walked past him without a word. Marius heard the click-clacking of her heels across Madame Millet's foyer floors as she headed out of the house. He did not turn around until she was gone.

Madame Millet waited for his attention with crossed arms and a half frown. Something inside him shrank at the sight of her disappointment.

"Inside, Mister Grey. Now," she said.

There was no arguing. In fact, the idea of arguing never

entered his brain. He followed Madame Millet into her office. He took a seat in one of the smaller armchairs while she shut the door behind them.

Madame Millet's office was actually another converted parlor. Those old restored homes seemed to be made mostly of parlors. This one managed to feel large and intimate at the same time. It was round with a circular table in the middle covered in colorful scarves. The walls were painted a pleasant shade of light blue with white edging.

All along the walls were books and trinkets and crystals. A few jars of fake voodoo magical things. Pickled hog ears in a fancy blue jar and a basket of stone eggs. These things were not totally worthless as far as magic went, but they were pert near.

"It's the only tasteful room in her whole house."

Marius tried to shush the voice underneath his breath as Madame Millet took her seat in the overstuffed chair across from him.

"Really, Marius? You really needed to pick a fight today?"

His shoulders slumped even further. A part of him wanted to shrink until he was small enough to hide inside the cushions.

"It's not my fault she's so uptight."

"Try again," Madame Millet said. "You were rude to your teacher."

Marius took in a deep breath and softened under her gaze. It was hard to fight her.

"I'm . . . tired, okay? I'm really just exhausted. I shouldn't have done it."

"If you need, we can help you. There are plenty of people who can go to your cemetery and do some chores or help you with the ghosts."

"No. I'd rather not."

"Why?"

"Because he doesn't want your nosy busybodies poking around in his things and finding all his monster-hunting stuff."

"Because it's my task to do. It's why the High Mystics pay me," he said quickly.

Madame Millet regarded him in silence. He let his eyes drift to the area behind her chair. There was a blue velvet curtain just behind her that hid a locked door. It led to her *real* magical stash. The good stuff. The strong stuff. She did not allow anyone back there.

"Are you sure that's all?" she asked.

"What do you mean?"

"Marius, I grew up with your mother. I know the signs. You come to school late and banged up sometimes. Two weeks ago, you had a limp you wouldn't explain, and today you look like you haven't slept in a week. You're not monster hunting, are you?"

Luckily, he did not have to fake surprise when he answered because she actually did surprise him. He'd had no idea Madame Millet suspected anything.

"She started when she was about your age, you know?

57

I remember thinking she was so cool because she went out monster hunting. When she came to school in a wheelchair, it changed my tune. But good ole Kelly did not heed my warnings. She went right back out as soon as she healed."

Marius was finding it difficult to speak. His mouth hung open for a while before he realized it.

"I'm not . . . doing that," he said numbly.

Marius did not elaborate. There was too much danger in that.

"You know, if you need money . . ."

"I don't," he said.

"All right. You are your own man. I will take you at your word. Just know I am here to help if you should need it."

Madame Millet opened her office door and let him leave. A part of him wanted to turn around and tell her. He wanted to tell an adult the real reason for what he was doing. He wanted someone to confide in, other than the voice in his head.

Nothing good came from trying to explain himself. Besides, Marius doubted Madame Millet would approve if he did tell her. Sometimes, she tried to mother him, and he hated when that happened. He only had one mother, and it was not her.

CHAPTER NINE

Marius sighed, feeling lonely. He never knew why going to school made him feel that way. Something about seeing all the other kids with parents to go home to. It reminded him of what he did not have. Plus, the conversation between Mrs. Pine and Madame Millet lingered in his brain.

There was nothing to do about it other than get to work. He had put it off long enough.

The path through the graveyard was mainly dirt and gravel until you got to the first grave. Then it moved into a cobblestone lane winding through the massive headstones. Each grave was a large pillar of white stone. Some had lovely carvings of crosses or flowers on them. Some were simpler and spartan. Most stood taller than Marius, allowing enough room to bury two family members, one compartment on top of the other. Every tomb was labeled with the family name.

In Louisiana, your family places your body in a tomb's compartment when you die. Then they wall bricks and replace the stone marker to seal you inside. In one year, the hot sun bakes you into ash, like a long, natural cremation.

When another member of your family dies, they brush your ashes aside to make room for the next body. In that way, you are always with your ancestors.

The problems occur when there are many deaths in a short period. Plagues are often the culprits. That is why the mausoleum wall was built.

A long wall that held three grave compartments tall and twenty compartments wide. It made room for extra family members and those who could not afford a family tomb of their own.

Marius walked the path through the graveyard. It almost resembled a little town with a road, each tomb an address. Put a few mailboxes along the path, and it would be the perfect neighborhood. Well, except for the lack of living people.

He took note of little things as he went. Some weeds were popping up through the cracks in the cobblestones, and a bird had taken to pooping on the widow Fermina's tomb again. Having the large cypress and oak trees about provided a nice atmosphere and plenty of shade, but it also attracted meddlesome birds.

At the end of the lane sat the largest burial site. It was a great mausoleum with its own wrought iron fencing. Spiked stone flowers garnished the top steeple. Rosebushes lined the gray-and-white stone of the building. *Family Tomb of Grey and Stone* was etched over the entrance.

60

If anyone dared to enter, they would have been utterly surprised to see a cozy home. The space was large enough to accommodate a family. There was one four-poster bed that had been largely unused since his mother died. It shared the same layer of dust as its matching dresser and end table. Cherrywood dressing screens partitioned the nicer furniture from what Marius used: a simple cot with an egg crate box in the corner.

A small refrigerator hummed away, plugged into a power outlet Marius's father had installed years ago. It was homey. Well, as homey as a mausoleum could be. All the decorations in the world would not hide the four rectangular grave markers in the back wall.

Marius took a minute to remember the way it had been. There were carpets, food, and people. A home with a mother and father. Lively conversation, music, and laughter. Marius's father adored reading books aloud to his family, while his mother preferred to tell tales of the monsters of the world.

"Oh, my dear Raymond. He loved all the books in the world. I mainly just loved the one."

"I put it in the safe, Mom. Your monster book will be waiting when you get back."

When she spoke, her voice seemed to echo in the empty mausoleum. He winced at the volume, even though he was pretty sure no one else could hear her.

"You get that from me, you know."

"What?"

"Only loving the one book. That was you too. Even as a baby. Your father used to get so mad at me for reading to you about ghouls and monsters before bed. He tried to sneak other books into your room. Tom Sawyer *and normal things like that. He finally gave up and bought you your own monster book. 'Cannot hold back the will of the tides,' he said."*

Now the other books were gone. The mausoleum was empty of conversation and laughter. There was only one bed made, and all the music had been put away.

The last time he had heard music inside these walls was over two years ago, when his mother used to sing. Those were sorrowful songs about missing his father.

"Why don't I miss him the way you do you?"

"You and your dad just never clicked like we did. Plus, you were so little when he disappeared. Not all grown-up like now."

"I'm only twelve."

"But an old twelve. Cemetery people are old souls. Not like your father. Such a young man, even for his age. I met him when he was twenty, but I didn't give him a second glance. Thought he was sixteen. He acted so young and unsure of himself."

"Mom, is he dead too?" Marius asked in a small voice.

"Why would you ask me?"

"Because you're dead, aren't you?"

"That's a difficult question, especially when you know the answer."

He sighed. This was always the end of the road when

it came to questioning his mother. No matter which way he asked, she stopped when she said, *Especially when you know the answer.* Anything after that would lead to utter silence, so Marius decided to switch gears.

Marius made his way to the cupboard. He rifled through the items until he found the miracle salve. It was mainly coconut oil with aloe and a basic charm on it, but it worked for sunburns and minor injuries. He rubbed it on his face and grabbed some water from the mini fridge.

The gardening basket sat in the corner of the room. Marius collected it and turned to leave. The upkeep of the cemetery was, after all, his responsibility. He had fallen behind in his duties last night and needed to catch up.

When he passed the grave marker on the far right of the wall, he stopped. Marius ran his fingers along the letters etched in cold stone. *Kelly Stone.* He traced three *X*s with his finger on her grave. It was the mystical world's version of saying hello to a dead person. It was also for protection and magic.

Nothing happened, of course. His mother's ghost was not in there.

He headed out into the cemetery with gardening basket in hand. First, there was the matter of the bird poop on the widow Fermina's tomb. She would have an absolute fit when she woke if he did not fix that. Then there was the matter of dandelions poking their yellow heads out where they were not wanted.

He was bent over, pulling the dandelions out of the stone cracks, when he heard a child's giggling. His head snapped up, but he saw nothing. Marius shrugged it off and went back to his work. There was a particularly large clump of weeds sprouting in between two of the older tombs. He sat up and reached for the trowel in his basket, but found it gone.

Another childish laugh filled the air. Marius scanned the area and spotted the trowel twenty feet away on a tombstone. He sighed heavily and rolled his eyes.

"I'm not in the mood," Marius said out loud.

He got up, rubbed his hands on his pants, and retrieved the trowel. When he turned back around, a boy was in his way, waving enthusiastically. Well, it was not really a boy. It was a ghost boy.

"What do you want, Hugo?" Marius asked.

"You didn't come home yesterday," Hugo said with a wry smile.

"Is that why you moved my trowel?"

"No. That was to get your attention," Hugo said.

"You have it, now what do you want?"

"I wanted to tell you that I won't tattle to the other ghosts. Not a peep from me, I swear."

"Thank you, Hugo. I appreciate that," Marius said with a fake smile.

Hugo had died when he was only nine years old and was buried in the cemetery alone. Orphans were not usual around the area since Lafitte and the surrounding towns were so close-knit, but Hugo showed up without any kin to call his own. When he died in 1910 of influenza, the townsfolk decided to bury him in the mausoleum wall out of pity.

Children buried without family tended to turn into lutins. Lutins were mostly harmless. Friendly ghosts who liked to haunt people in order to play games. Hugo was particularly fond of hiding Marius's tools and making mischief.

The main difference between a lutin and a regular ghost was that lutins ventured out in the day. Regular ghosts could not leave their graves until after dusk.

Hugo appeared to be so excited to see Marius, he kept flashing his image in and out of focus.

"The widow asked about you, but I didn't say anything. The widower too, but I didn't say anything. When Father Clifford and Abigail asked . . ."

Most of the time, Marius did not mind the lutin. It was like having a little brother who never aged. Right now, everything was just a little too much. He was tired, and his sunburn hurt. His patience was not up to its usual level.

"Let me guess. You didn't say anything," Marius snapped.

He felt instantly bad about it when he saw how Hugo's ghostly expression fell. It was not nice. After all, Hugo was the only ghost in the cemetery that knew about his monster hunting. The lutin had caught Marius thumbing through his monster book one day when the others were asleep.

Despite all of Hugo's silliness, he had never ratted Marius out to the other ghosts. Not once.

Marius did not tell the ghosts about his other life for the same reason he kept it from most people. They would intervene or pester him. They might find out his plans, and he had so little time left.

"I'm sorry, Hugo. I didn't mean it. It's been a long couple of days," Marius said.

"Aw, that's all right. Hey, did you catch something?" Hugo asked, his spectral eyes wide with renewed excitement.

"A boogeyman."

"Really! Oh, I bet that was fun. Was he all like—*pow pow*! And I bet you were all, no way—*bam bam*! And then you were the best, and you won."

Marius smiled. One of Hugo's favorite things were the comic books Marius brought home. He liked the ones about superheroes the best, so he imagined every monster battle looked like the comics.

"Yeah, buddy, I won," Marius said. He didn't have the heart to tell the lutin that the boogeyman was only worth a measly ten Mystics.

"That's so cool. You're so cool," Hugo said. "I didn't rat you out."

"I know, buddy. I know. Here. Why don't you sit with me while I weed this section and tell me about what all I missed."

Hugo floated excitedly over to the patch of weeds. Marius listened intently as he talked about all the gossip. Madame Quincey did Abigail Fisher's hair again, which made Father Clifford really angry. The Watt siblings, Evaline and Rickie, found a baby bird that had fallen from a nest, and they argued as to who should replace it. After a lot of bickering, Athena Barber finally let Nellie Ross babysit little Elvis so she and her husband could have a midnight stroll alone.

Before they knew it, the sun was setting in the west. The rest of the ghosts would rouse soon, and that meant only one thing. A trip to Mama Roux's Cajun Kitchen for a big family meal. It was hard to tell which one of them was the happiest about that prospect.

CHAPTER TEN

Marius's stomach grumbled as he took a head count of the ghosts gathering around him.

At the front of the line was Hugo, followed by Rickie and Evaline Watt. The Watt children were aged fourteen and fifteen, respectively. Next was Madame Quincey, who had been a fancy courtesan in her day. Behind her stood Rolland and Athena Barber, Athena with baby Elvis on her hip. The spinster, Nellie Ross, and Widow Fermina clustered together. The widower Mr. Stevens stood close behind them.

As usual, Father Clifford and his adopted daughter Abigail cut to the front of the line so he could berate Marius. It was his favorite evening pastime, and one that made poor Abigail extremely embarrassed. She had died when she was only thirteen. The optimal eternal age to be forever embarrassed by your parents, as Abigail liked to say. She held back, pretending to talk to Hugo.

"Where were you last night, dear boy? We nearly sent a search party," Father Clifford said in a blustery voice.

"I was indisposed, sir," Marius said.

He fought extremely hard against talking back to the ghost. After all, what kind of search party could the ghosts possibly send? They could not leave the cemetery without him. Marius bit down on his tongue so as not to point that out. Arguing would just delay dinner.

"Indisposed? I dare say we should be your top priority!"

"You are, Father. But there was a little girl in need of help," Marius said, hoping he would not pry further.

"And there was no one else to help her?" Father Clifford asked.

"No, sir."

"You are but twelve years old. I find it hard to believe someone older could not ..."

Marius noticed the smallest break in the water's surface just offshore. It happened so slowly most would not have seen it. The top of a round silhouette in the bayou water lit in the fading sunlight.

Only Marius recognized it for what it was. Not a log or a turtle. It was the top of a mermaid's head.

Rhiannon must have been listening. Father Clifford's voice did carry. Marius looked out to where she was and shook his head ever so slightly. He was not able to see her eyes, but he hoped she got the hint. Whatever she did, Rhiannon could not let anyone see her. Not even the ghosts.

"All right, everyone," Marius said loudly, interrupting the priest. "Everybody is here. Let's be off to dinner."

Marius walked forward, leaving Father Clifford in his wake. The ghosts chatted happily and followed him along the worn path out of the cemetery. Not all ghosts came out of their crypts at night. Some did not believe themselves to be dead, so they stayed in the place where their ashes rested.

Others were too old. They gave up their ghostly spiriting long ago and preferred to seep into the rocks and plants around them, forever a part of the earth. Either that or they moved into the next stage. The great beyond. The afterlife of their choosing.

Marius led the procession of spirits up the trail, across a walkway made of garden stones, and straight to Mama Roux's Cajun Kitchen. It was not a normal restaurant. Mama Roux's was a place for the living and the dead. Both ate there. That was the only reason to build a restaurant so close to a graveyard. The High Mystics paid her extra to entertain the local spirits.

As far as Marius knew, no one had ever seen one of the High Mystics. He wondered if they were a myth. The cash stacked in his safe was the only sign the strange council was real. For his cemetery work, they paid him in human money. Every month a small sum just appeared in his safe. No explanation and no messenger. Just *poof*.

Holding the back door open, Marius counted off the ghosts as they filed inside. One by one, they passed him with excited faces. Even Father Clifford lit up amid the colorful ambience of the restaurant.

Fish baskets and Christmas lights hung from the ceiling. Pictures of people posing with fish they caught covered every empty inch of wall space. There was an entire wall near the bathroom devoted to those Billy Bass plaques that sang when you pushed a button. Raucous zydeco music filled the air. It was hard to hold a sour face in Mama Roux's.

Marius took in the smell of the heavy air filled with fried food. He had not eaten all day, and Mama Roux had the best fried shrimp in the world, as far as he was concerned. No sooner had he escorted the ghosts into the dead dining room than a large woman swept him up in a tight hug. Marius found himself enveloped on all sides with Mama Roux's love.

"Oh, mon petit! I missed you so much. I was so worried when I didn't see you yesterday!" Mama Roux said in her thick Creole accent.

"I can't breathe," Marius said after squeezing her back.

"Sorry, child," she said, letting him go. She patted his hair, trying to smooth it. "I was worried. You hafta tell your Mama Roux if you're gonna miss supper."

"I'm sorry, Mama Roux."

"Well, dat's okay. You want you a shrimp basket?"

"Yes, please," Marius said.

Talking with Mama Roux always felt like talking to a grandmother. There were times he wished she would invite him to stay at her house again. A place he could live forever. A home that looked like any other home with a sofa

71

and a TV and a real bed with blankets that smelled like dryer sheets.

Mama Roux did ask him once if he wanted to live with her. It was right after his mother died. He told her no because of one important reason. Marius was going to get his mother back, and to do that, he would have to hunt monsters the way she used to. Mama Roux would never permit hunting in her home, so he declined her offer without her ever knowing why.

Mama Roux smiled grandly at him, a round woman with a huge grin. Her eye shadow was always either green or blue depending on which outlandish dress she wore. Her hair was dyed bright auburn and fashioned into that older woman Afro that so many southern women reverted to in their golden years.

"I'll get that for ya. Sit there. I will get you a Coke too," she said, pointing to a table in the corner.

Marius took his normal seat and scanned the patrons. There was a living dining room and a dead dining room in Mama Roux's place. His ghosts went into the dead dining room, obviously.

Even though they did not need to eat food, some still liked to pretend. Mama Roux had a trunk full of fake food for them to play with. Wax fruit and wooden bread painted to look like the real thing. It made them happy.

In the living dining room, humans ate the real stuff. There were the townspeople who were seemingly unaware of the supernatural world. They drifted in for lunch and dinner. If they ever noticed the strange cemetery boy holding a door open for a long amount of time for no one at all, they did not say so.

Mama Roux would often let the ghosts mingle with the living diners. After all, they were invisible to most people, so moving around the restaurant undetected was easy. They especially loved sitting in empty seats next to real people, smelling the food they ordered and pretending to talk with them. Hugo smelled Marius's food all the time.

All knew to steer clear of any tables with children. They were the ones most likely to spot a ghost. Kids were still open enough to see them. They had not lived in the human world long enough for it to convince them ghosts were made up.

The other people, the ones that existed in between realms, ate in the living dining room as well. That was Marius and Mama Roux. A few other people came and went. Psychics and voodoo people. Madame Millet was known to visit the place from time to time. Sometimes creatures stopped in—ones that could conjure a realistic disguise. Demons, mainly.

The High Mystics had strong opinions on monsters. Such beasts were beings hell-bent on murdering people. They ate either human flesh or human souls. Monsters were not to be tolerated.

Demons, on the other hand, fell into a gray area. They did not murder. They merely struck deals. Crossroad demons were especially sneaky about that, but no one was harmed that did not sign on the dotted line.

People wanted all manner of things. If they sold their soul to a demon, they could get what they wanted. When that time was up, there was nothing for it. The demon collected. The High Mystics let that slide because of the choice in the matter. Hey, the human did not have to strike the bargain in the first place, did they?

Marius had just started shoving fried shrimp in his face when he spotted Rex across the room. Rex was a crossroad demon, and a particularly nasty one. He wore a pin-striped suit that was perfectly pressed, and a hat that resembled one of those old mobster ones from the 1920s. When Marius made eye contact with him, he smiled wide like the Cheshire cat.

"Don't pay him any mind, petit," Mama Roux said, placing a Coke in front of Marius.

"Why do you serve him here?" he asked with a grimace.

"This is a neutral place. You know dat," she said.

They watched Rex stand and greet a frightened woman as she entered the dining room. She was painfully thin under a dark dress. She wore some sort of wrap around her face and head and kept to the shadows. It was impossible to see her face. The poor thing looked desperate, wringing her hands and sweating down the neck of her dress.

Marius watched her slip a wad of money across the table to Rex, but he shook his head no. He handed the sweaty bills back to her. The woman got up and ran out of the restaurant crying.

"I don't like it any more than you, child. Poor thing thought she could buy more time with regular money," Mama Roux said.

"Did he even bother telling her she could pay it off with Mystic coins?" Marius asked.

"What's the point? Regular folks can't get ahold of those."

"Yeah, I guess."

Mama Roux placed a warm hand over Marius's shoulder. He broke his gaze away from Rex to meet her eyes.

"You ain't got those coins, do you?" she asked, looking worried.

"Just a few from when Mama was alive. From when she used to hunt," he said.

"I just heard things, petit. I heard you might be doin' something foolhardy like monster huntin'. You ain't though, are you? You tell Mama Roux the truth now. I hope you ain't lettin' anyone wind you up in somethin' dangerous."

Marius took a deep breath and let it out through his nose. He softened his eyes and relaxed his shoulders. Lying to Mama Roux was not something he liked doing, but if he did not, she might interfere. She was sweet and worried after him. He hated lying to her.

"I promise, Mama. My nose is clean."

CHAPTER ELEVEN

When Marius opened the door to the Habada-Chérie, Madame Boudreaux was nowhere to be seen. The shop did not smell of frankincense for once. It was nicer. Maybe lilac? Perhaps this was what Papa Harold liked, and he only got his way when the old crone was gone, he thought.

"Welcome, young Marius," Papa Harold said with an open smile. It reminded Marius of a withered jack-o'-lantern that had been left out too long. "I hadn't expected you back so soon. What can I do for you?"

"I need another job," he said without so much as a greeting. Marius thought better of it and added, "Please."

"Another one? But you were just here with the boogeyman. Already you want another bounty?"

Marius shifted his weight and fought not to look down at his shoes. He hated showing his cards. He hated showing anyone that he *needed* something.

"I . . . want more. The boogeyman didn't pay well enough. Do you have anything bigger?"

Papa Harold grimaced. "I see. Well, I bet I can find something for you."

The grizzled shopkeeper tried for another grin, but it was much smaller than before. He gestured for Marius to follow him, and they ventured through the hall and back to his room.

Papa Harold produced a book from underneath his table. He opened and thumbed through it, licking his fingers between each turn of the page. Marius decided to sit rather than stand awkwardly by the door.

"Things have been a little quiet," he said without looking up. "But there are rumors of a rougarou in one of the bayous. It chased some hunters and scared the buzz out of a drunk fisherman."

"I can't do that one," Marius said.

"Right you are. Rougarous are quite a task. All those teeth. Even the best are wary of those," he said absently.

Papa Harold turned a few more pages, scanning the columns with his rosy, pointed fingernail. Marius stared at his painted hands. He never could understand why a person would take the time to get fancy manicures.

He stopped about halfway down the page. Another gruesome smile spread across Papa Harold's face.

"I hear rumors of a candy lady in the quarter. That might be up your alley," he said. "You are good with the kid's room monsters."

"I can do a candy lady. Is that all? Any more on the list?"

"Just a generic candy lady. Would you like the info?" Papa Harold asked.

"Yes, I'll take it," Marius said.

Papa Harold tore out a column from his book and placed it on the table. Marius pulled his monster book from his coat and opened it to the first blank page available. With careful fingers, he lifted the slip of paper and dropped it on the open book. For some reason, it reminded Marius of offering Rhiannon a fish.

It was possible to capture monsters without a bounty. As long as you had a monster book and the right words, any monster was yours to cage. Accepting a bounty gave you an advantage. Any intel your employer had transferred to your book. Last seen whereabouts, spy observations, hunting ground perimeters. All of it made the monster hunter's job that much easier.

The book's page glowed brightly as it consumed the torn bit of information. When the glow subsided, the words *Candy Lady* were written across the top. Marius stood up and thanked Papa Harold, bowing a little as he made to leave.

"Be careful, child," Papa Harold called after him. "Candy ladies are tougher than they sound."

CHAPTER TWELVE

One of the perks about being a cemetery boy was the ability to travel through graves. Since Marius was only twelve and had no parents to escort him in a car, he had no choice but to walk everywhere. It would have taken him ages just to make the trip to Madame Millet's house and back entirely on foot. He was always late enough to school as it was, and that was with the grave hopping to the Holy Name of Mary Cemetery near Madame Millet's house.

Marius was able to enter any grave, think of where he wanted to go, and transport himself into that very cemetery. It was a mildly terrifying task if you were not used to it. To transport, you had to crawl into the small hole meant for a body and pop out of the other side. The journey was dark and dirty, but Marius was so used to grave hopping, it never bothered him.

Luckily, when grave hopping, cemetery people moved through bricks and gravestones like they were not there. And the magic of grave hopping never moved them through a new tomb. Crawling over a still-rotting body would not be a pleasant experience.

Today, however, he had to go farther away. Marius had business in the French Quarter of New Orleans. That meant hopping to St. Louis Cemetery No. 1.

The problem with going to that cemetery was that it was always very crowded with tourists during the day. Marius preferred to make his journeys there at night because it was closed to visitors, but that was not possible today. He had far too much to do and extraordinarily little time to do it in.

Marius walked just outside the arched sign of his cemetery. There stood one of the oldest tombs in the area. If there had been a ghost in residence, they'd never showed themselves to him. Their burial grounds had become dilapidated before he was born. He had pried the headstone away and removed the bricks long ago.

"Oh, Marius. Grave hopping again? It's far too dirty. Your clothes."

He had been right about to crawl inside when her voice popped up and scared him. There just had to be some warning system they could use.

"We don't have the car anymore, Mom. Remember, you wrecked it."

"I was killed in it. Such a mouth, Marius. Are you really blaming me for that?"

"No, Mom. Sorry."

"Don't take your frustrations out on me. It looks ugly on you."

He had a quip on the tip of his tongue, but he bit it back. After all, the crash had not been her fault. She did not want to die in an accident. His mother never meant it to happen.

However, there was another side to that coin. A side that was her doing. A deal she made that set everything in motion. But he would not think of it. Not right then. He had work to do.

Marius rolled up his long sleeves and crawled into the grave. He thought about St. Louis Cemetery No. 1, picturing it in his mind. He made his way to the back of the grave and through to the other side. The bright light of the day blinded him as he tumbled through the grave and onto a well-kept stone pathway.

Marius stood up and dusted himself off. Immediately, he regretted his timing. Five school children in uniforms gawked at him. Their teacher was nowhere in sight.

Oh great, he thought. Now he would have to come up with a story. There was one in particular that always worked with kids.

"Who disturbs my slumber?" Marius said in a weird, shivering voice normally reserved for bad movies. "Why have you awakened me?"

The children gaped wide-eyed at Marius. Two of the girls held each other. One of the boys slid slowly behind the group. He looked like he was trying to run away but without the others seeing.

"Answer the question, or I will curse you to the farthest trenches of Hell!"

Marius's voice boomed, and he placed a hand on the gravestone next to him. It made the tombs around the children vibrate. They all jumped with loud shrieks and ran away.

Marius relaxed. The ghost bit worked, but he'd really lucked out in that none of the children had phones. That would have complicated matters. The last thing he needed was his picture taken.

He took a deep breath, got his bearings, and headed out of the St. Louis Cemetery No. 1. It was a winding, twisting cemetery full of tourists, but Marius knew it well. He always hopped into the Italian section because tours rarely went there. Somehow, he managed to make his way to the exit without running into the curious school children again. Now it was time for supplies.

The first stop was the St. Louis Cathedral in Jackson Square. The square was always bustling with music and life. Artists, musicians, and street performers were everywhere. Tourists clamored to take in the sights and get their palms read. People painted like silver statues scared kids who dared to offer them money. The smell of sweetness filled the air.

Marius splurged and bought a bag of beignets, resulting in a mess of powdered sugar on his hands and coat. He did not care. There was nothing better than fried dough when you were hungry on a beautiful day.

After cleaning himself up, he visited the cathedral. It was a beautiful church, and one Marius chose because it was often crowded. Tourists were good for some things, and he counted on their help now.

Marius grinned when he saw a group of well-dressed people insisting on all of their tour guide's attention. Wealthy people who wanted the royal treatment. The guide's words were loud enough to draw others closer. As the mass of people grew, the clergy flocked to them like mosquitos to a bug zapper.

He followed a group of slightly drunk people inside, hiding in their numbers. When they accosted the first priest with questions, Marius peeled off.

He made his way to the water-filled stone bowl by an altar of the Virgin Mary. After checking to see that the tourists were sufficiently distracting, Marius removed a small flask from one of his pockets and filled it with holy water. Then he pulled three rosaries from his other pockets and dunked them in the bowl. One was particularly special, so he made sure to soak it thoroughly.

Marius almost got away with it. Had he been just a tad quicker, he would have. When he turned to leave, he found himself face-to-face with a priest. His heart leaped into his throat, and he readied himself to bolt.

"What are you doing here?" the young priest asked in a whispered hiss.

When Marius got over his shock, he realized the clergyman looked familiar. Yes, he knew him. Marius managed to breathe again. He was safe after all.

"Duncan, you scared me," he said.

"Scared you? You scared me! I saw someone stealing holy water and thought I'd have to, like, attack you or something," the priest said nervously.

"Like you would attack anyone," Marius said with a smirk.

"I might. You never know," Duncan said defensively.

Duncan was, by all accounts, a coward. He was twenty years old and extremely unsure of himself. Basically, the priest had no backbone and a shiny yellow streak down his belly. After Duncan got a look into the supernatural world of ghosts and monsters, he lost what little nerve he had in the first place.

When Marius first met Duncan, he was hiding under a pew from a pair of baby gargoyles. Normally, gargoyles haunted the rafters and bell towers of churches, turning to stone when anyone happened to spot them. If someone thought they saw a movement in the corner of their eye, the doubts quickly disappeared when they came face-to-face with an unmoving statue. Marius heard Paris was infested with them.

Poor Duncan was locking up the church one night when a pair of babies climbed down to get a better look at the young priest. They did not know any better. Duncan shrieked and ran screaming.

Marius just happened to be pilfering some holy water at the time and coaxed Duncan out. They watched the mother gargoyle carry her babies away. Duncan was never the same after that.

Marius liked Duncan for two reasons. He was an over-all well-meaning guy, and he treated Marius like a hero. No matter what Marius did, Duncan covered for him. He had it in his head that Marius had saved his life that night.

He had no intention of telling Duncan that the gar-goyles would never have hurt him. They were gentle things. But it was nice to have a priest in his corner.

"What are you doing with that holy water?" Duncan said.

"I just need a little. I wasn't going to take much," Marius said.

"And those," Duncan said, pointing to the rosaries.

"They are for a friend," Marius said after quickly stuffing them in a pocket.

"I should turn you in," Duncan whispered.

The priest looked around wildly. As far as subtlety went, Duncan was a bull in a china closet. Marius tried not to roll his eyes. He remembered what his mother had said about how someone could be young or old for their age. Duncan was an adult, but he acted so much younger.

"Come on. Let me go. I have a candy lady to hunt," Marius said in his most convincing voice.

Duncan's face fell. All the color drained from his skin. Marius thought he could see the priest's lower lip quivering with fear.

"What . . . what's a candy lady?" Duncan asked.

"Do you *really* want me to tell you?"

There was a long pause where neither Duncan nor Marius said a word. They stood together in silence while the priest thought hard about his answer. When he finally spoke again, his voice came out a little woozy, like his lips were numb.

"No. No, I don't think I do."

"Then can I leave?" Marius asked. "I don't have long to find her before . . ."

"Before what?" Duncan asked.

"Trust me. You don't want to know."

Marius was laying the danger on thick. He knew if he scared Duncan enough, he might let him go. Candy ladies were not pleasant, but it was not like he was going up against a rougarou or anything.

"Okay. Okay. Hurry out the front. I'll cover you," Duncan said.

Marius turned and bolted for the door. Duncan threw a happy smile on his face and greeted a new group of tourists. He moved them in front of the other clergy so no one saw Marius leave.

The monster hunter walked out into the bright light of

Jackson Square with a smile on his face. Music filled his heart and street performers danced around him. Oh, how he wished he could stay awhile and revel in the fun. Rhiannon was not the only one lured by the world beyond her own.

Alas, he had to leave. His next stop was the most important one.

CHAPTER THIRTEEN

Papa Renard's store was a few streets off the grid. It was in an inconspicuous place. A modest storefront set in between a laundromat and a corner grocery. The one window Papa Renard owned was decorated with simple, innocent-looking items. Candles, incense, and a few gris-gris dolls that could have come out of any souvenir shop on Bourbon Street.

There was a symbol known to all who lived between worlds. It was a skull with an *X* for each eye and one *X* for a mouth. The number three was sacred, and so was the letter *X*. Three *X*s in a skull's face meant you dealt in real magic. Papa Renard painted his skull just above his door in white.

Marius walked into Papa Renard's shop. When the door opened, a high-pitched howl sounded from overhead. That was what they used instead of a bell. Papa Renard told everyone it was the recorded voice of a griffin.

Griffins were supposed to ward off evil with their call. Marius was dubious. Griffins were reported to be extinct.

To him, it sounded an awful lot like Mama Roux singing over a boiling pot of crab.

He made his way through the tourist items in the front until he reached the counter in the back of the store. There sat Papa Renard himself. He wore a top hat and smoked an old pipe. The smoke coming from it smelled like cloves and rose hips. His head was freshly shaven, showing off the serpent eating its own tail tattoo on the back of his neck. He turned to address Marius with a genial grin beneath a heavily waxed mustache.

"Marius Grey. What do I owe the pleasure?" Papa Renard asked.

"I need some supplies," Marius said.

"Is that so? Well then, what can I get you?"

"A dozen chicken feet, black salt, ground honeycomb, and some cat claw's bark."

"What are you looking for, young Mister Grey? Other than the chicken feet, these here are the makings of a tracking spell," Papa Renard said.

"I'm after . . . a candy lady. I hear one was lurking near here."

Telling an adult about hunting was a gamble. Most considered him too young. Others stayed out of his business. It was hard to tell on which side of the line people would land.

Marius hoped Papa Renard would fall in the leave-him-alone camp. It would be so easy for him to report Marius to Madame Millet.

"You know, I've heard tell of something along those lines," Papa Renard said. "Mrs. Krishner over on Port Street, her boy woke up with four of his teeth missing. Poor child was so ill he had to be hospitalized. I will throw in some finely ground charcoal."

Marius let out the breath he was holding.

"Thanks. Over on Port, did you say? Okay, I can start there," Marius said.

"Hold on now. We should discuss payment. Four jars of your good graveyard brick dust should about do it," Papa Renard said, gathering the ingredients Marius requested.

Marius had two impossibly deep pockets on the inside of his trench coat. One always held his book of monsters. The other held various ingredients too large or cumbersome to fit in a normal front pocket. The pockets held most of the weight of the objects, so he was not bogged down all the time. When he peeked inside, he realized there were only three jars of brick dust. He took them out and lined them along the counter.

Quickly he patted his other pockets for more things to barter. His hand grazed two possibilities. There was the Mystic coin he'd earned for the boogeyman, and the three rosaries he had just blessed at the church. Marius took out the rosaries and placed two on the counter.

"I think I said four jars of brick dust," Papa Renard said flatly.

"I know, but I only brought three. I can also throw in

these rosaries. They were just christened an hour ago in holy water from St. Louis Cathedral."

"That's a start. How about the third one you put back in your pocket?"

Marius stiffened. There was little Papa Renard did not notice. He ran the carved beads under his fingers.

"It's for a friend. Not up for barter," Marius said.

"Fair enough. What else do you have?"

Marius sighed heavily. He had about twenty dollars of real money on him, but that would not be enticing to Papa Renard. He would want something far more valuable than that. Slowly, Marius pulled the Mystic coin from his pocket and set it on the table. The number ten glistened in the shop's light.

"Well, now. That *is* worth something," Papa Renard said with his eyes glowing.

"Will this cover me?" Marius asked.

"And then some," Papa Renard said with a smile. "You can take back your rosaries. I have more than I can sell at the moment. And take some of those worry bracelets and extra chicken feet if you like."

Papa Renard placed all of Marius's items in a bag and handed them over. The two shook hands. When they did, the slightest spark lit between their touching palms. The light was the faintest shade of blue. Both nodded and smiled to each other.

It was the way of things. Magical transactions were

sacred. Often, they were a barter situation. Both parties needed to make the trade in good faith. After a barter, the two people shook hands. If the spark between them was blue, all was well. If the light was black, it meant someone was lying.

"Thank you, Papa Renard," Marius said.

"Happy doing business with you."

Papa Renard took Marius's brick dust and Mystic coin in the back storeroom. A beaded curtain rattled as he drifted through it. As soon as he was gone, a pale boy stuck his head around the corner of a display case. It was easy to spot the black, frizzy hair next to the white candles and birchwood boxes. Marius went over to him.

"Hey, Antoine. Did you get what I asked for?" Marius asked.

Antoine was Papa Renard's son. He was not good at hiding his feelings. No poker face, as Marius's mother would have said. It did not help to have powerful and strict parents. Antoine fidgeted nervously.

"Yeah, I got it, but . . ."

"But what?"

"My mom will kill me if she ever finds out I shared this."

"Well, then I will use it to resurrect you again," Marius said with a smile.

"It's not funny. Have you read this before? It's powerful

stuff. How are you even going to save up enough Mystics for it?"

"That's my problem," Marius said, eyeing the piece of paper in Antoine's hand.

"Are you sure? I mean, this spell has to be done within two years of someone's death. It's been almost two years since your mom . . ."

"Don't you think I know how long it's been? Come on, Antoine. We had an agreement. You get me that spell, and I won't tell your parents about that thunderbird egg you are trying to hatch in your attic," Marius said. "Look, I even got some chicken feet from your dad."

Marius reached inside the bag Papa Renard had given him and pulled out half of the chicken feet. He handed them over to Antoine.

"Make a circle around the egg with these, and it will entice the bird to come out. You don't want to be stealing Papa Renard's stash. He counts everything," Marius said.

Antoine took the feet with a nod. With a shaky hand, he reached into his pocket and handed Marius a folded piece of paper. Marius felt the warm weight of it in his hands, and it gave him a good measure of comfort. One less thing on the list. One less ingredient to gather.

Marius stuck out his hand and shook Antoine's. When their hands met, a sickly green light fired. It shocked them both a little, and Antoine jumped away. The spark was not black, but it was not clean either. Marius stared daggers at Antoine and held out his hand.

"All of the spell. Hand it over. You promised," he said.

"I'm sorry! I just don't feel good about this," Antoine said, darting his eyes around the room. "I had to dig it out of her books in the safe. It's super dangerous. It says they don't always come back ... right."

"Yeah, I'm aware. I'm also aware that we had a deal."

Marius set his jaw and held his hand out. Inside, he kicked himself for trusting Antoine this much. It was a stupid mistake. There was only one living thing he could count on, and she was swimming in the Mississippi.

Antoine looked sheepish. He reached for a pocket in the back of his pants and brought up another sheet of folded paper. As soon as he handed the slip over, Marius took it and stormed out the door.

CHAPTER FOURTEEN

Had Marius been smart, and not as angry, he would have stayed at Papa Renard's place and borrowed a mortar and pestle to mix the ingredients together for the tracking spell. That would have been the right thing to do, but Antoine had made him so mad, he walked out without thinking. His pride was too big to let him go back inside, so he decided to grind the ingredients together in a recyclable coffee cup he got from the corner store.

After the tracking powder was mixed to his liking, Marius headed to the neighborhood Papa Renard had mentioned. Along the way, he came across a Lutheran school, and decided to drop his first pinch of powder. A candy lady would start where children congregated.

Marius tossed a pinch of dust here and there. If powder lit up in one direction, it meant his monster had been that way recently. There were tracks all around the school, but they were older. She had probably found a victim and followed them home. The dust glowed brightest at the southeast corner of the school, so he went that way.

It was getting late, and more people were coming home from work. Several had to sidestep him. Each looked at the peculiar boy like he might be insane. Most didn't seem to notice he existed until they were nearly on top of him. Between his grayish complexion and ability to move effortlessly into the background, Marius was almost like a ghost.

Men rarely gave him a second thought. The ladies were a different story. Their faces turned into expressions of question and concern. Marius shrugged it off and grinned at the strangers. Smiles were great tools for disarming the nosy.

Had he been a normal kid, he would have gone to a normal school too. There would be a record of him in some office file cabinet. Paper trails, birth certificates, emergency contact numbers. People would have taken him away when he was orphaned.

He was a cemetery boy on no one's radar. Undocumented in the normal world. But he had to stay that way, so he smiled at passing children and said, "Good afternoon," to the ladies.

The tracking powder glowed brightest down a particularly cozy street. Every house was a different color. Blue, red, purple. The shutters on the windows were equally vibrant. Marius listened carefully and heard the sound of children giggling in the air. This was a neighborhood filled with kids.

There was a good chance the candy lady chose it as a hunting ground.

Marius moved like a ghost around the houses, as quietly as he could. Small communities like these noticed outsiders. Tourists did not come to these parts often, and a new boy lurking around would be suspicious. Unfortunately, he had to get in close.

"Check the windows."

"I'm going to check the windows, Mom. I was just about to," he whispered through gritted teeth. She always chose the worst times to start talking to him.

"That's where they like to leave the candy for the children."

"Mom, stop. I know this already."

"All right, smart-mouth. What are they, then? You know everything. What are candy ladies? Come on, we haven't done a lesson in a while."

"Not here. There are people around," he said.

"Not close enough to hear very well. Quit stalling, big monster hunter. Tell me what they are."

Marius breathed out the deep exhalation only a frustrated son can accomplish. No one but his mother had the ability to bring it out in him. Apparently, she did not even need to be here in person. Her voice was enough.

"Candy ladies can be a number of things," he began, making sure not to move his lips too much so passersby did not see him talking to himself.

97

"That's all you got?"

"Some are the ghosts of women looking for their children. Others are jilted tooth faeries who grew up to be angry old women. I know the stories, Mom. You read your monster book to me so many times. Why are you grilling me?"

"Because you missed the last alleyway and didn't even think to check that rosebush for sugar and calcium deposits."

Marius stopped and sighed heavily. She was right. He had totally missed all of that.

"You're slipping."

"No, I'm tired!"

His voice carried more than he intended. Marius sucked in his breath and looked around to see if anyone heard him. There was no one in sight, so he was in the clear.

"There are kids in danger."

"I know," he said, feeling defeated.

"The rosebush, son."

Without another word, Marius checked the bush. No sugar or calcium. He peeked down alleyways and jumped a few fences with renewed focus. Most windows were barred, but some were left alone. It was not until he got to his fourth alleyway that he spotted the candy on the windowsill.

"Bingo."

Marius heard children arguing inside the room. It was hard to tell how many. There, on the first-story window, sat a handful of candy. Not store bought. No labels anyone might recognize. It was not like candy ladies bought their goodies. An assortment of peppermint sticks and taffy wrapped in wax paper made up the little bundle on the window.

It was a good find and made all the better by the fact that it sat untouched. Candy ladies are known for haunting streets, placing candy on the windowsills of little children. If one of the kids takes the candy, they unknowingly invite the candy lady into their home. Then she can enter in the night and steal their teeth.

Marius quietly took the candy from the windowsill and put it in one of his pockets. These children had not invited her in, but he was not about to leave the temptation there. If he took the candy instead, there was no way she could be invited inside. These children would be spared.

He skulked through the neighborhood, looking for more candy. After finding the first bundle, it was easy to follow the trail. Marius spotted five more resting untouched on the windowsills of children's rooms. Either the kids in the neighborhood knew the superstitions, or they were smart enough not to take a stranger's candy. Marius pocketed each bundle he came across.

When he came to the house with the purple shutters, his stomach dropped. The window nearest the fence had recently been disturbed. Marius saw paint chips missing from where the screen had been removed and then replaced. When he peeked inside the curtain, he spotted a small boy sucking on a peppermint stick wrapped in wax paper.

Relief and dread filled Marius's body. It was an odd feeling to be sure. There was a relief when a hunter found the next victim before they became a victim. Marius now knew where the monster was going to strike. However, he also hated the fact that something terrifying was about to happen to this poor kid.

Marius stuck his finger in the tracking dust and drew three Xs on the wall outside the boy's room. The letters lit up brightly, confirming the candy lady had lingered here for a long time. He took a deep breath and looked for a place to hide.

He could not sit out in the open. Even if the candy lady did not care, the neighborhood people would. Someone would surely call the police. The best solution was to hide in the child's room, like he had with Violet's closet, but there was no time for that. It took a lot of stealth and planning to do something like that.

The best Marius could find was a gathering of unpruned shrubs against the fence. He crawled inside on hands and knees, curling up in a ball. Lying in the dirt was not pleasant, so he curled his arm underneath his head to act as a pillow. The bushes gave him cover, but he also had a clear view of the boy's window.

Marius had no intention of falling asleep, but somehow, he managed to do just that. Something about the sound of the crickets in the night, and the rustling of the leaves overhead. Maybe it was because he was so bone tired lately. Sleeping in boats and hunting around the quarter wore him plum out. Either way, Marius fell asleep and did not wake up until the whole world was dark.

"Marius! Marius, wake up!"

CHAPTER FIFTEEN

He startled awake. It was dark. After realizing his error, Marius sat up and pulled himself out of the collection of bushes. A tremor shook his rib cage as he picked the twigs and bugs out of his hair. He gaped around him but saw no one. Then he noticed the window. It was opened, and the screen was removed.

Marius flew to the window and looked inside. There stood a terrifying woman dressed in all black. The candy lady looked like she'd just come from a funeral. A pale, solemn-looking figure. Her skin was sallow, and her hair hung loose around her shoulders. You would never know she was a monster. She looked like a creepy woman, but a human woman all the same.

It was not until she moved that the monster showed itself. She crawled like a spider from the foot of the little boy's bed to where he was sleeping peacefully. Her movement was short and jolting, like she had mechanized joints malfunctioning from disuse. She jittered her way until she was face-to-face with the boy. The candy lady knelt over his legs and smiled down at her victim.

Marius readied his book in his hand and tested the window. He would need to raise it higher to fit through. It creaked a tad, and the candy lady whipped her head around to investigate. Marius ducked behind the wall. Luckily, she did not see him.

Marius would have to be fast. The window was going to give him away pretty quickly. He had to jump in the bedroom, capture the candy lady before she could run, and get out without anyone hearing. When he popped his head back up again, he saw a sight that was undeniably horrifying.

The candy lady had peeled off the skin of one arm, exposing green, swampy flesh beneath. When Marius peered inside, she was removing the skin from the other arm. She stood up on the bed and shimmied out of the woman's flesh like she was getting out of a tight-fitting dress. Last was the face. The strangely human face of the candy lady gave one last smile before the creature underneath ripped it off like last year's Halloween mask.

The creature left standing was made of green sinew and bones. Veins of moss and blood residue clung here and there under her arms and down her ribs. Her face was little more than a skull with the slightest of lights inside her eye sockets. A black mass of moss and vapor encircled her head like a floating cloud of undulating hair.

It was a boo hag.

A boo hag was far more dangerous than a regular candy lady. They were monsters who were best not trifled with. They lived on violence and the life energy of humans, especially children. When a boo hag sucked you dry, there was nothing left of you. You were drained all the way down to the calcium in your bones.

Marius's heart thudded hard in his chest, and he lost his nerve for a minute. Something deep down in his veins told him to yell for help and run away. It was cowardice, pure and simple. It would have been something Duncan would do. Maybe what Antoine would do. No, he told himself. There was no running. He could not leave that boy alone.

He looked back over the window and saw the boo hag crouched over the child. Her black talons clutched the sides of his twin bed, causing the mattress to creak. The poor boy was just waking up to see the face of violence and death above him. When he opened his mouth to scream, she opened hers as well.

His scream caught in the air between them before the sound ever made it out. Her terrible black skeletal mouth opened wide and began sucking the light from the boy. The child's life force came out as dazzling white light. When it entered her body, it glowed inside her ugly green chest, lighting her from within.

Now was his chance. The monster was distracted. Marius threw open the window and jumped inside the room.

The window screamed loudly when he did, but the boo hag did not respond right away. She was far too busy with the boy, so Marius gained enough time to reach for his brick dust and throw it in her face. He may have come up short with Papa Renard's trade, but Marius always had some stashed away in an emergency pocket.

The boo hag wailed and broke her connection with the child, but she did not back away like the boogeyman had. Instead, she wiped the dust from her hollow eyes and turned on Marius with a low grumbling growl. The sensation in Marius's spine went cold as the boo hag jumped off the bed and faced off with the young monster hunter.

The little boy was unconscious. Not dead. Marius saw his chest rising and falling. That was a good sign, but most of the boy's life force was now glowing inside the chest of the horrifying boo hag. It was a brilliant light shining between protruding ribs.

She moved closer, seeming to grow taller with every step. Her emaciated face turned this way and that as though she was taking his measure. Marius grabbed the flask of salt from one pocket and drew a crude circle on the floor with it. His hands were shaking as he reached for the book.

"What have we here?" the boo hag said. "A baby hunter? Marius Grey, if your book's cover is to be believed."

With every word, the child's life force beat brighter and brighter. She took another step closer, careful not to touch the salt. When the boo hag breathed out, the odor of decay followed along. It smelled like rotten food and stagnant water. The sickening stench of a carcass left out in a bog to rot and putrefy under the humid sun.

"I'm here to stop you and save the children of this neighborhood," he said, trying to sound big and brave.

Marius whipped the book open to the proper page. The binding hummed with the promise of caging another monster. When he spoke again, it was deep and confident.

"Grab the arm, grab the crook. Stomp the ground until it's shook. Invisible line, invisible hook. Get the monster . . ."

Before he finished, the boo hag reached out a long, clawed hand and slapped the ground hard. The floor rumbled beneath his feet and he dropped his book. It crashed to the ground, skidding across the line of salt. Marius looked in terror at the clean break in his salt circle. Now that the circle was broken, there was no protection for him.

The boo hag seized her opportunity and grabbed Marius by the neck. She dragged him away from the corner and threw him roughly to the ground as far away from the salt as she could. All the wind flew out of his chest when his back hit the floor. Marius gasped helplessly for air.

"Not much of a hunter," the boo hag said as she climbed over the top of Marius. "This coat with all your spells will not save you, child. But you will taste good, I am sure."

Her sharp nails ticked and scratched the wooden floor as she moved over him. Marius tried to scream, but nothing came forth. Her terrible face met his, and he stared into her ghastly, sunken eyes. Everything smelled of rot and ruin. Carnage and decay.

Marius quickly reached for his pocket with the brick dust, but the boo hag was quicker. She clawed open his hand so fast he saw the blood before he felt the pain. Three cuts sliced the top of his hand from thumb to wrist. Marius winced and tried to pull away, but the boo hag pinned his shoulder down with one massive hand.

There was only one last move to make. Marius pulled his knees to his chest and kicked upward with his feet. The stunt did not give him much room to work with. The boo hag was large and heavy, and he was not able to shift her much. Luckily, it was just enough to make his move.

He took his injured hand and ripped open the top buttons of his shirt. There hung his mother's talisman. A silver-coated raven's skull with the charmed moonstone. It was always there, attached to his neck with a chain of pure sterling silver. He was not sure exactly what it could do or what magic brought it to life, but monsters seemed to hate it. When the long-distance barriers failed, he always had the talisman.

When the boo hag came face-to-face with the raven's skull, the moonstone glowed brightly. It cast flashes of silver light around the room, bouncing off her gnarled face. She flew off Marius and scrambled away across the floor.

"What have you got, baby hunter?" the boo hag grumbled, pointing at the talisman.

Marius stood tall with the skull in full view. The moonstone glowed as he neared the creature cowering on the floor. She moved back farther and screamed when she unwittingly ran her claws across the salt on the floor. He took the opportunity to attack.

With a swift motion, Marius reached into his pocket and brought forth his short fillet knife. It was always razorsharp. He leaped forward and plunged the blade into the boo hag's chest, right in the middle where the small boy's life force was held. Her scream came out as a gargle. Her body emptied of the stolen energy. It drifted into the air of the room like blue vapor and flew back into the boy via his mouth and nostrils.

The child sat up abruptly, looking wild-eyed around the room. He gaped at Marius standing over the writhing boo hag, his knife sticking out of her chest. The boy opened his mouth to scream but stopped when the hunter put up his hand.

"Don't yell. Not yet. Not until I capture her."

For some reason, that worked. The boy shut his mouth and watched. He trembled all over beneath his blanket. The boo hag moved helplessly on the floor, trying to right herself. Without the stolen energy, she was significantly weaker. By the time she stood up, Marius had the book in his hand and was pointing it directly at her.

"Grab the arm, grab the crook. Stomp the ground until

it's shook. Invisible line, invisible hook. Get the monster inside this book!"

The force from the pull nearly knocked Marius over. Even though he'd weakened the boo hag, she was still five times stronger than your average boogeyman. She clawed at the floor, stretching her body away, but there was no fighting the spell. A monster book, wielded by the right spell, could overpower anything.

With one last grumbling snarl, the boo hag left the mortal plane and was sucked into the pages of Marius's book. He shut the cover, and at last, the world went quiet.

CHAPTER SIXTEEN

As far as Marius was concerned, regular human parents made extraordinarily little sense. He had fought boogeymen, candy ladies, poltergeists, and now boo hags in children's bedrooms for almost two years. For some reason, a lot of monsters flocked to children. In all that time, he had noticed that parents rarely responded to creepy noises in their children's rooms with any regularity.

One time, a boogeyman made such a racket, Marius could have sworn the whole neighborhood would come rushing in to see what was wrong. Other times, a few creaking boards were enough to bring in a helicopter mother. It seemed the older the child, the less likely it was that anyone would check on them. Also, if the parents were into wine after dinner, they often left well enough alone.

But there was one surefire way to call a parent, even the worst parent. A child's tears. It flipped the parenting switch into hyperdrive. Whether it incited anger or sympathy, they still came running.

The boy began crying. It took a little bit before Marius heard it. His ears were still ringing from the force of the magic. The child's whimpers turned into cries, and his cries turned into sobs. Marius was across the room and on the bed next to the boy in seconds. He placed his uninjured hand over the boy's mouth.

"Shhhh. Now, listen. I'm Marius Grey, and I hunt monsters. I tracked this one to your room, and I came in to help you. I need you to help me. Please don't cry."

Two dark eyes peeked over his hand, water still rimming their edges. The boy's terrified, injured soul was barely hanging on. After a long minute and some silent coaxing, the child nodded slowly.

"Okay, good. I'm going to take my hand away. You are going to be quiet so we can talk, right?"

Another nod. Marius removed his hand. The little boy's lower lip quivered, but he did his part. He did not cry.

"What's your name?" Marius asked.

"Henry," he said quietly.

"All right, Henry. You did really good. Very brave. I'm proud of you. Now, I'm going to take my book and leave out of your window. I need you to promise you won't tell anyone about this. Not ever."

"How come?" Henry asked.

"Because they will never believe you," Marius said simply.

Henry gaped at Marius but eventually bobbed his little

head. It was the plight of all children, and most children knew it from experience. Adults never believed you.

"What are you gonna do with her?"

"I'm going to take her to a place far away," Marius said, holding the book tightly with his injured hand. "It's kind of like a prison for bad things. Evil monsters get sent there forever so they can never hurt good kids like you ever again."

The pages of his monster book were still glowing green. It shivered under his grasp and bucked against him. Marius clenched down, even though it felt like his hand was on fire. He was able to keep a straight face for the kid.

"Even dads?" Henry asked.

"What?"

"You said there's a place that's a jail for monsters . . . so they can't hurt kids like me. Does that mean dads?"

This took Marius aback. He stared into Henry's watery eyes for a long time before he saw the scars beneath them. It was not fair, and it was not right. This was not the first monster this kid had seen.

"Is your dad hurting you?" Marius asked.

Henry shrank into his pillows and curled in on himself. Marius's book bucked again, harder this time. The wound on his hand was really starting to hurt. Had Henry's words not engulfed all of Marius's spare attention, he would have broken and shouted in pain.

"I . . . I didn't say that," Henry said.

Marius fought down the red-hot lump in his throat. This was almost worse than the boo hag. Monsters were monsters. It was their nature to do evil to humans. But a father? They were never supposed to become monsters. They were not meant to hurt, or to vanish for that matter. He suddenly wished he could capture Henry's dad in his book and cart him off with the boo hag.

The book bucked again, and this time Henry noticed. Marius sucked his breath in pain. The poor kid's face filled with terror all over again.

"She can't get out, can she?"

"No. It's just a stitch in my side. Fighting with her took it out of me. Here, help me with the window, would you?" Marius asked.

Henry followed him off the bed. The plain truth was the boo hag should not be able to get loose. The binding in the book kept her wrapped up tight, but the fight she was giving was real. She was still so strong, and he was injured. It felt like she was trying to claw her way out. That could not happen, not in front of sweet, scared Henry.

Before he jumped out of the window, Marius decided to do one last thing for the kid. He reached into his pockets and produced a rosary and a bracelet of worry beads. With one hand, he put the rosary over Henry's neck and the bracelet on his wrist.

"What's this for?"

"These are worry beads. If you feel anxious or are afraid

at night, spin the beads in your fingers and tell them what's bothering you. It will take your worries away," Marius said.

"And the necklace thing?"

"It's a rosary, recently blessed. Wear that around your neck for protection from . . . from any other monsters that might be in your house."

A long moment passed between them in which the book bucked again. Luckily, Marius had stuffed it in one of his inner pockets so Henry could not see. The pain in his hand screamed to be acknowledged. He bit the inside of his lip to hold it in check.

"But . . . we ain't Catholic," Henry said.

"Doesn't matter," Marius said, patting him on the head. "It's a protection. Doesn't matter the faith. If the blessing of the thing is genuine, the power will be too. This will protect and hide you from monsters."

Henry stood a bit taller. It was as though the items gave him new powers. Marius knew that was not the case. They were protection, plain and simple. They gave no powers, but why not let the kid think that. It did not hurt. In fact, it could help make his own power.

Marius climbed through the window, waited to hear Henry lock it behind him, and then ran like a bat out of hell. The boo hag was fighting to get free from inside the book. He felt her hatred heating up the binding. With every shriek inside the book, another shot of piercing pain stabbed at his hand. There was a wriggling under his skin, like something was alive inside. With every movement, new agony blossomed along his nerves.

He had no choice, he had to pull out the book in public. There was nothing for it. He had to bind it together or else she would break through and finish what she started. Marius's head swiveled up and down the streets. There seemed to be no one around.

When he pulled the book from his coat, it was already an inch open. That should have been impossible. Monster books had binding spells built into every fiber of their being. Every stitch, every drop of glue was bespelled to hold the evil creatures inside until they could be weighed and processed. Yet, there was no mistaking the black talon trying to pry open the book from within.

Marius pulled another rosary from the coat. He threw the book down on the ground under a streetlight and touched the beads to the boo hag's claw. It retreated back inside the pages, but she did not stop trying to open it. Marius took the rosary and wrapped it around the book itself. It seemed to hold her at bay just enough, but with every cry she shrieked, a fresh pain shot in his hand. When he inspected it, what looked like a thorny worm wriggled underneath.

Terror shot through his body. This was far more than he had bargained for, and there was no one nearby to help him. Papa Renard's was way too far away, and Madame Millet's house was on the other side of the river.

The river. He was not far from the river. Only a few blocks maybe.

Marius held the book against his chest with both arms. The rosary was holding tight, but he was not sure for how long. He turned his nose in the direction of the Mississippi and ran as fast as he could away from Henry's house.

Please let her be there, he thought. *Just please.*

CHAPTER SEVENTEEN

Marius made it to the river. It was not easy.

There was no way to just hop into the river from that side of town. There was a stone wall separating the neighborhoods from the water. Luckily, someone had left their boat and trailer parked at the end of the street, and Marius was able to use it to hop over the floodwall. From there, he had to cross several railroad tracks, dodge some drunks on the Cres Park Trail, and jump a fence.

When he was finally able to wade into the murky waters of the Mississippi River, he grabbed a handful of ground jasmine from his coat pocket and threw it as far as he could. There was no snared fish to tempt her with, but he hoped the jasmine would be enough.

He tried not to think about how unlikely it was that she would be nearby. The river was huge, and it emptied into a million little bayous and causeways, like the one that led to his graveyard. Wanting Rhiannon to be near enough to help was a pipe dream, but it was his only hope.

"Mom?" he said to the empty air.

The fear crept down his spine with every stab of pain. Terror and loneliness fought for control over his body.

"Mom? Please say something!"

Nothing. Not a word. He was going to die here in the Mississippi alone. Torn apart by a boo hag he could not handle.

The water came up to his waist. Even though the inside pockets of his coat did not get wet, his trousers could. He felt the warm, muddy water soak his socks and fill his shoes. The book kicked against his chest, but he held on despite the searing pain in his hand. Marius shut his eyes, doing everything in his power to focus on calling out to Rhiannon through the jasmine in the water.

"Marius?" said a small, girlish voice.

His eyes flew open. He had been tensing so long, he did not notice that Rhiannon was right in front of him. Her large aquamarine eyes took him in worriedly.

"Rhia? You're here?"

"Yes, I heard you. What has happened?"

She took his hand and led him deeper into the water. There was a place between some sunken trees that was more private. Even though very few people frequented the walking trail at night, it was better to hide as much as they could.

Rhia threaded a few long fingers in between his arms and tried to unravel the book from him, but it bucked against him. Instinctively, Marius squeezed the volume tighter. Hot tears were gathering in the corners of his eyes. There was just too much pain.

"What is going on? Marius, speak to me."

"It was a boo hag. Papa Harold sent me to collect a candy lady, but it wasn't just that. It was a boo hag. I caught her, but now she won't stay inside! I've never seen this before. She keeps clawing back out."

The creature thrashed under his skin again, and Marius flinched in pain. It seemed to be growing. Every wiggling jerk scraped against his tendons and bones. He nearly dropped the book. Rhiannon grabbed his hand to examine it.

"You are injured? Did she hurt you?" Rhia asked, her face full of concern.

"She clawed me when we were fighting. Now there's . . . something . . . inside me."

Rhiannon's look became so focused and intense, Marius was afraid. It was the way predators appeared in the wild right before they lunged at their prey. That steadiness of muscles, the dilation of the pupils. Marius watched in horror as Rhiannon opened her full, flesh-eating mouth. She stared down hungrily at his hand.

"Marius, she's going to eat you. Pull away!"

"Rhia, no! Wait!"

In a flash, Rhiannon's serpent tongue licked out from between her razor teeth. It dug deep in Marius's open wound. He screamed in pain as her tongue wrenched this way and that, tearing at his flesh while grappling with the creature inside. With a terrible ripping sound, Rhiannon retracted her tongue from his hand. Marius nearly fainted from the pain and loss of blood.

"Ouch! What the . . ."

The mermaid dangled what looked like a small eel from her tongue like a fisherman proud of their catch. The creature was black and greenish with knobby wrinkles and two bony talons. It wriggled in Rhiannon's grasp but did not get free. She pulled it into her great, toothy maw and snapped her mouth shut. As soon as she did, the book stopped fighting him and fell still.

Marius clutched his hand to his chest. It still hurt. A throbbing pain rose and fell with the beating of his heart. When he inspected the wound, it was bleeding profusely. Perhaps he was mistaken, but the scratches had not bled much before then. Now that the creature was out, the wound wept blood easily.

"Boo hag scratches embed pieces of themselves inside you. She was able to fight your book because there was still a piece of her out here," Rhiannon said.

Her mouth was back to normal, but Marius noticed she was still chewing. To anyone in the world, she would pass as a young girl, wading in the water and chewing on bubble gum. They would not be able to fathom the fact that she was grinding the corpse of a boo hag's worm in her sharp teeth.

"Ummm...thank you," Marius said woozily.

The world shifted in and out of focus. His head seemed light and dizzy. His vision spun as the lights across the river blurred.

"Whoa there," Rhia said, grabbing ahold of his arms. "Don't faint on me. We need to bind your wound. Here, be still and give me your hand."

Marius held out his hand to her. In the back of his mind, he wondered if she was going to eat it the way she had eaten the creature inside it. After all, mermaids never had allegiances to humans. His mother's voice sure thought the worst. Yet, they were friends. Despite all the odds, a boy and a mermaid were allies. He tried to remember that in his haze of fear and blood loss.

"Hold your hand up high like this," Rhiannon said while lifting his hand in the air. "It will help with the bleeding."

She reached into his pocket and removed his knife with a casual movement. It struck him suddenly that she knew which pocket held it. She did not root around or anything. Rhiannon brought the blade to her hair and cut off a long lock. Marius gave over his hand numbly as she wrapped the hair around his wound.

Instantly, the pain subsided, and the bleeding stopped. It took a long minute, but Marius regained most of his faculties. He was able to see straight again, more or less. At any rate, he was not going to pass out, and that was an improvement.

Marius examined the makeshift bandage. Mermaid hair consisted of strong filaments held in place with a fine kelp-like sheath. Rhiannon's was nearly white, and the bandage she made shone iridescent in the moonlight.

"Thank you, Rhia. I didn't know that mermaid hair could do that."

"It's not something we like to advertise," she said quietly. "Otherwise, hunters would be butchering us left and right. Our hair can bind just about any wound. When you're done with it, just wind it around a fish bone and it will keep fresh if you ever need it again."

"I don't know what I would have done if you didn't show up to help," Marius said with a good helping of relief in his voice.

"Probably died," Rhiannon said plainly.

Marius screwed up his face and stared at her. Then he remembered mermaids were not great at subtlety. It was not like Rhiannon could practice talking to humans. He was the only one.

"How did you get here so fast? I thought it was a long shot you'd be nearby."

"I followed you," she said.

"How? I grave hopped. I was on land."

"You have an odor I know really well. I can smell you from pretty far away," she said.

"I have an *odor*?" he asked.

Marius was not sure how he should feel about that.

Without thinking about it, he raised one of his arms and took a quick sniff. He made an immediate note to apply deodorant as soon as he got back home.

"Yes, like grave dirt and seafood. It's nice," she said.

"Ummm . . . thanks?"

"You're welcome."

"At any rate, I'm glad you were here," Marius said.

"We are friends," she said with a smile.

"We are. I wish I could stay, but I have to get this book to the Habada-Chérie and collect the bounty. The boo hag may be contained for now, but she was powerful. I don't want to chance her getting out."

Rhiannon lowered her head, obviously deflated. Marius felt a pang of guilt. She came all this way to help him, and now he was running off again.

"We can hang out afterward, okay?" he said.

"Hang out?" she asked with a confused look on her face.

"Yeah. Like we normally do. Talk and stuff. Just meet me back at the graveyard dock. I'll be there in a few hours."

Her aquamarine eyes lit up again, and she smiled.

"Okay! I can do that."

"I won't have time to grab you a fish," he said.

"That's all right. I ate an alligator for lunch and then another one for dinner. Still pretty full from that."

Marius spared a moment to picture Rhiannon battling with an alligator. Its teeth against hers. The poor creature did not have a chance.

"Two hours," Marius said.

"Yes, I'll be there," Rhiannon said. "I'll probably eat again before then, just in case."

She turned to swim away, when Marius remembered something important. He reached for her hand with his bandaged one. Remarkably, it barely hurt anymore.

"Wait. I almost forgot," he said, pulling the third rosary from his pocket. "This is for you. I got it blessed today."

He'd saved the nicest one for her. It was made of small rosewood beads. Each one was intricately sculpted to resemble a skull and sealed with varnish. The cross at the bottom had a pattern of swirling fish etched into a metal inlay. It had cost him five Mystic coins from the Habada-Chérie.

The heavy cost was worth it to see her face when he held it out to her. Rhiannon's eyes sparkled in the dim light as she took in the necklace. When she failed to take it from his hands, Marius reached out and placed the rosary around her head. It fell around her neck.

"This will keep you off other hunters' radar. It's for protection and concealment. As long as you don't kill any humans, they should forget you exist."

Rhiannon held the necklace with the reverence of a praying nun. She opened and closed her small mouth several times before words came out.

"You really are my friend," she said quietly.

"Of course," he said. "I don't want you to get hurt. You're my best friend."

Marius did not mean to say it. The words came out without his knowledge. He never honestly thought about what they were to each other. Yet, it was true. As soon as the words flew out, he knew they were right. His best friend in the whole world was, in fact, a flesh-eating mermaid.

CHAPTER EIGHTEEN

It took several wrong turns into unknown neighborhoods and some creative grave hopping to make it to the Habada-Chérie. The blood loss made him clumsy, and he landed in his home cemetery a few times. Of course, the fact that it started raining did not help matters.

To get to the store, Marius had to grave hop into the St. Francis de Sales cemetery. Normally, it was a pleasant enough place to go. There was a huge mausoleum that was climate controlled and everything. Compared to his little home, it was a mansion.

The problem was a hurricane had ripped through the area months ago, knocking out the giant skylight. It still was not fixed, and rain poured down through the open hole in the ceiling. Moonlight illuminated the spot where the rainwater pooled on the mausoleum's floor. The sight looked holy, like there was something sacred about rain falling among the dead.

Marius saw no ghosts, and sensed nothing sacred at all.

He was wet and tired. When he passed through the moon-light, he just felt like a drowned rat.

By the time Marius opened the door to the Habada-Chérie, he was barely standing. His clothes were soaked, and he was covered in grave dust. Madame Boudreaux laid eyes on him and immediately stuck out her tongue in disgust.

"What fresh hell chewed you up? You look like yester-day's cat barf."

Marius did not respond. He merely pushed past her and headed for Papa Harold's room.

"Hey, gross boy! You can't go tracking that mess in here!" she called after him.

All of Marius's attention was directed ahead of him. He focused on getting to the back room, getting paid, and going home. The sooner he finished his business, the sooner he would be floating in his little boat, listening to Rhiannon sing him a lullaby. Even the marrow in his bones felt tired.

As luck would have it, Papa Harold was seated in the back room. He was reading some book with odd pictures on the front, which he quickly shut and stowed away when Marius approached. He gaped down at Marius, taking him in.

"What in blue blazes happened to you?" he asked.

"It wasn't a candy lady," Marius said flatly.

Papa Harold stared at him for a minute. He took in the state Marius was in and gestured for him to sit down. Marius did so without a word.

"Let me get you a towel," Papa Harold said slowly.

The tall man disappeared and came back with a towel. Marius was not sure how long it took. Time moved so strangely when he was this tired. All he knew was that it was long enough to soak the cushion beneath him.

Papa Harold draped the towel around him carefully, and Marius pulled it tight around his shoulders. The air-conditioning on his wet skin made him shiver.

"What do you mean it was not a candy lady?" Papa Harold asked.

"I mean what I said. Here, see for yourself," he said, plopping the book on the table with a loud *thunk*.

It still jumped a little and vibrated when his hand moved closer. For a minute, Marius was worried that maybe there was still some trace of the boo hag in his hand. Perhaps Rhiannon had missed a bit. Thankfully, the book did not open.

Marius felt a tad jumpy now that he was facing off with Papa Harold. He was a nice enough person, but the mermaid hair was still wound tightly around his hand. He concealed it with a strip of fabric ripped from his shirt. When Papa Harold locked eyes on it, Marius pulled it back underneath the table.

"Don't let him get his hands on that. It's only inviting trouble."

Luckily, the shopkeeper did not pry further, even though his eyes kept tracking back to Marius's hand. He merely got out his scales and took the book.

"You want to tell me what it was, then?" he asked.

"A boo hag," Marius said quietly.

"What? No. That can't be. All my scrying and the reports pointed to a candy lady."

"Well, it wasn't. It was a boo hag pretending to be a candy lady. She put out candy like one and everything. I saw her peel the candy lady skin off before she sucked the life from a little boy," Marius said.

He spared a brief thought to the skin left behind. He could not remember if it had still been there when he left or if it got sucked inside the book as well. There was too much going on.

Papa Harold's expression went from disbelief to fear. His eyes squinted at Marius.

"I've never heard of a boo hag using a candy lady for a skin."

"Me neither, but it's true," Marius said.

"Is he . . . the boy . . . is he dead?" Papa Harold asked in a whisper.

"No. I saved him," he said.

"It's good you were there, then."

"I wouldn't have been. I would never have taken this job if I'd known," he said.

"My apologies, young Mister Grey. All my intel said she was a candy lady. I would never lie to you about that. I provide the jobs, and this is my mistake. You are quite the hero in my book."

"Can we just weigh this? I want to go home," he said, staring at the scales.

"Sure thing."

They moved through the regular routine. Papa Harold put the book on the flat scale. He moved metal weights this way and that. Once the proper weight had been measured, the copper penny glowed brightly. It grew into the shape of a fully formed Mystic coin. The number one hundred was printed on the top.

"That was quite a payday," the shopkeeper said.

"Yes," Marius said with a long sigh. "It nearly killed me, but yes."

"Well, you must have someone watching out for you," Papa Harold said.

Marius smiled inwardly. If only he knew who was looking out for him. It was more than a little funny that Marius's guardian angel was, in fact, a carnivorous monster in the shape of a thirteen-year-old mermaid.

"You know, since you are moving up in the world, I do still have that rougarou in the swamps," Papa Harold said offhandedly.

"Are you kidding?" Marius asked.

He never could get a good bead on the man. One minute he seemed concerned for Marius's welfare. The next, he was suggesting dangerous missions that could kill him.

"Don't look at me like that. You proved yourself against

a boo hag. Maybe you are ready for bigger and scarier things."

"I nearly died!" he said with more hysterics than he had anticipated.

"But you didn't, Marius. Look, I'm not here to tell you what to do. I'm just going to tell you what I know," Papa Harold said, rolling up his sleeves. "I don't know what you are saving up for, but you are saving for something big. I've seen you in here with small bounties ever since your mother passed, God rest her soul. A rougarou is a big score. Much bigger than a dozen boogeymen at least. If you want the job, I'll give it to you."

Marius glared at him for a long moment, not really knowing what to say. He clutched his book in one hand and his new Mystic coin in the other. Luckily, the book no longer hummed with the energy of the boo hag. Her life force was gone. She could hurt no one else.

"This is my faith in your abilities talking," Papa Harold said when it was clear Marius was not going to speak. "You don't have to do it, but the offer is there."

"Thank you, but I'm passing," he said.

"That is your right. Now, go home, young Mister Grey. You look plum tired. There's an ungodly amount of jambalaya left in the kitchen. Help yourself but return Madame Boudreaux's Tupperware this time. She nearly chewed my hide right off."

Marius thanked him and left the room. He half expected to see Madame Boudreaux waiting on the other side of the door with a wooden spoon or something to hit him with. Thankfully, there was no one. Just an empty hallway that led to an empty kitchen that led to an empty night.

He helped himself to two large servings of jambalaya. One for him and one for Rhiannon. Even though he was exhausted, the least he could do was offer his savior a proper meal. Two alligators or no, Rhiannon was always hungry.

CHAPTER NINETEEN

Two days later, Madame Millet's house loomed in front of him. He did not want to be here, and judging by the hissing cats, they did not want him here either. Had Marius not missed a ton of school already, he would have just stayed home.

There was a fine line between absent and truant. Absent could be explained away with chores or an illness. Truant was call for Madame Millet to pay him a visit. A powerful priestess poking around in his stuff was the last thing he wanted. What if she found the spell? What if she saw Rhiannon?

Marius shuffled to the door, trying to hide his limp. He was not too late. Maybe only a few minutes. Before he could pull open the door, it was flung open to reveal a familiar, unwelcome face.

"You're late again," Mildred said, stepping in front of his path.

Marius had to stop abruptly so as not to slam into her.

Mildred crossed her arms over her chest. There was that cruel smile of hers again. Marius was fairly certain she lived to torment him.

"I'm not in the mood, Mildred. Let me by."

"But I have something for you," she said.

"What could you possibly have for me?"

With a quick motion, Mildred blew a pinch of dust in his face. It was hard to tell exactly what it was, but it smelled of talcum powder, honeysuckle, and glitter. She giggled as he lolled backward. Her words came in a singsong voice.

"Scary Faery, tongue and cheek. Doesn't our Mary look awful weak?"

Marius suddenly felt tired. It was that fatigue one felt all the way into their guts. He had been tired a lot lately, but this hit him harder. It was like a dense fog rolling over his mind. Luckily, he had enough wherewithal to understand a shallow spell when he heard one.

He reached into his top left pocket and pulled out a handful of brick dust. Not just any dust. Marius's brick dust was the best because he collected it from his own graveyard. He mixed it with a little graveyard dirt to add to the potency.

Cemetery brick dust was strong enough to break most spells and hurt most monsters. Mildred was not technically a monster, but it would still suit his purposes.

Marius threw the brick dust in her eyes, and she snapped back with a small shriek. She grabbed at her face. Instantly, the sleeping spell evaporated, and he could see clearly.

Mildred held her hands over her eyes, spitting dust on the floor.

"How dare you!"

"Didn't anyone tell you not to play with fae magic, Milly?" Marius asked with a laugh. "They are such fickle creatures."

He stepped past her. Mildred grunted and swiped blindly in the air where he should have been. She was angry, snorting like a beast. Marius whistled a little tune as he passed her and headed for the classroom.

He was seated at his desk before the lesson began. Mildred came in soon after, rubbing her eyes and pouting. Marius knew she would not rat him out. If she did, she would have to explain the fae spell. Her maman was not a fan of faery magic. Too volatile.

Madame Millet stood in front of the class with a wide grin on her face. The rebuke Marius expected never came. She barely noticed him at all. He breathed a sigh of relief.

"Welcome, class!" Madame Millet said excitedly. "Today we are going to go over some crossovers in history."

Marius rolled his eyes. So that was why she was so happy, he thought. Madame Millet simply adored talking about history.

"What do I mean when I say crossovers?"

Three hands shot up. It was no big surprise they belonged to the triplets. Before Madame Millet had a chance to call on anyone, they all started talking at the same time.

"A crossover is when human history and magical history..."

"Stop it! I know it! It's when they overlap—"

"I can tell it better! The two histories affect each other!"

Madame Millet's eyes widened as she waited for the trio to finish elbowing and taunting one another. When things quieted, she continued.

"That's more or less correct. But next time, let's wait until I call on you."

"Sorry, Madame Millet," they said in unison.

She nodded and reached for a book on the desk behind her. It had several bookmarks in the pages. Madame Millet opened to the first one.

"Let's start with the French Revolution of 1789. Can anyone tell me what magical event actually sparked that conflict?"

"The Great Gnome Wheat Wars!" Shirley and Ramona said in unison. They did not even bother raising their hands.

The teacher sighed and shook her head.

"That is correct. Well, mostly. Gnomes call it the Great Gnome Wheat *Dispute*. They feel *war* is a tad too aggressive. Which is ironic because their poisoning of one another's wheat led to a great famine, which sparked the French Revolution. That was a *very* aggressive period of history."

Shirley and Ramona slumped in their seats, deflated about their error.

"Here's another one. The Mongolian sorcerer's uprising

of 1195 led to what famous figure coming to power in the normal world?"

"Genghis Khan!" Ethan said.

"Correct. Khan was actually the only sorcerer left standing after the uprising. He used the souls of his fallen brethren to prolong his life and vitality. In fact, he is still alive to this day. Emperor Lizong of the Song dynasty in China imprisoned Genghis Khan inside a statue. It's walled away in a secret chamber inside the Great Wall of China."

The class was interrupted by the sudden intrusion of Mrs. Pine. She barged into the room looking a mess. Her hair was a ratty pile and her eyes were red-rimmed. Somehow, she had managed to lose more weight since the last time Marius had seen her.

Everyone stared at her, and she seemed suddenly very aware of her appearance. She sniffled and held a handkerchief to cover her face.

"Charlotte? Are you all right?" Madame Millet asked.

Mrs. Pine shook her head. Her eyes pinched in a painful way.

Madame Millet wrapped her arms around Mrs. Pine and led her away from the class. The math teacher began sobbing and whimpering. Her words were loud enough to hear before they got to Madame Millet's office.

"I did it, Madge. I had to. The doctors said nothing else could be done."

"What happened? What did you do?"

"I can't tell you. He said I couldn't . . ."

Their voices faded away, leaving the classroom eerily still and quiet. Marius sat in his chair, thinking about the terror in Mrs. Pine's voice. He supposed the shoe was on the other foot now. It was his turn to pity her.

CHAPTER TWENTY

The days calmed for a short spell. Marius went a whole week without monster hunting. It was a week where he showed up to school on time. A week where he got good rest. Also, it was a week where no one saw Mrs. Pine.

Marius spent his time outside of school working in the graveyard or chatting with Hugo. The deep gashes on his hand started healing up. He took care of his ghosts, escorting them to dinner every night the way a good caretaker should. Even the ghost of Father Clifford lessened his evening battery of complaints.

Even though things were calming down in the cemetery, Marius still could not make himself sleep in his cot in the Greystone tomb. He visited in the daytime to drop off supplies or bring in groceries that would spoil outside the refrigerator. Every visit ended in him marking his mother's grave with the same three Xs, but he never stayed to sleep. It was just too ... empty and cold in there.

Instead, he chose to take a pillow and blanket to the boat

outside of the cemetery. Every evening, Marius anchored in the middle of the bayou, and every evening, Rhiannon came to visit. They talked and laughed. When Marius began to drift, she would cling beneath the boat and sing a song to help him sleep.

Sometimes, he managed to hook a fish during the day to give her. Other times, he begged some fish parts off the cook at Mama Roux's Kitchen. Marius knew the mermaid was capable of fending for herself, but it made him feel better to offer her something.

Marius felt happy for the first time in a while. He was a hundred Mystics closer to the cost of the spell, and things were looking up. That meant he was about fifty from his goal. Bag a few more boogeymen or a real candy lady, and that would be more than enough. It would take a dozen poltergeists, but those were easy.

He needed sleep and food. His body screamed at him to slow down, so the monster hunter finally decided to listen.

Marius's stomach was full, and his days were filled with purpose. He had gentle dreams instead of nightmares while sleeping in his boat. The conversations with Rhiannon and Hugo drifted away from monsters and onto other topics. Nicer topics. Ones that did not involve blood and claws.

Of course, like all things, happiness comes to an end.

Thursday night, he led his pack of ghosts over the hill to Mama Roux's Cajun Kitchen. Nothing was out of the ordinary. The widows gossiped, Father Clifford huffed and puffed about this or that, and Hugo skipped along, chatting excitedly. Apparently, Mama Roux had bought a new set of fake food. There were wax grapes and carrots now.

The skull with the three *X*s was carved inconspicuously in the frame of the back door of the restaurant. Marius touched it for good luck. Then he plopped down at his favorite table and let Mama Roux play with his mop of hair as she talked.

"Oh, petit, what I wouldn't give to take a set of clippers to dis mess. You are handsome, but think of how gorgeous you would be if we cleaned dis here up a bit."

"Maybe later, Mama Roux," he said with a grin.

"Shrimp basket again for you?" she asked.

"Yes, ma'am. Please."

"Comin' right up. You are finally gettin' some meat on your bones. I like what I see."

Mama Roux moseyed away, calling for a shrimp basket from the kitchen as she did so. Marius grabbed his Coke and sucked down half of it in one long pull. Today had been a hot one. He was feeling overly cheerful until he spotted Rex, the crossroad demon.

Rex leaned against a corner, looking out at a woman pacing back and forth through the dining room windows. He chewed on a toothpick as he watched her. His eyes narrowed, and a smile spread across his face. The woman could not see him, but he tracked her like she was prey.

Marius recognized the poor soul who had tried to pay the demon off with cash money. The woman moved here and there, somewhat aimlessly. She would make for the door of the restaurant, and then turn away. It was as though she could not make up her mind. Would she come in or would she leave?

Marius took her in. She was thin, entirely too thin to be healthy. Her dark complexion was almost gray in the full moonlight. Bags hung heavy from beneath her eyes. It was the eyes that caught him. Those large, dark eyes. They reminded him of Henry, the little boy the boo hag almost killed. She could very well be his mother with a resemblance like that.

Then it hit him. When she stepped under the light, and her head wrap fell off, he got a better look. *How could he not recognize her before?* he wondered. That jittery walk and her thin frame. It was Mrs. Pine.

"Here's your food, petit," Mama Roux said, setting a basket of fried goodness in front of him.

"What is that woman doing here?" Marius asked, pointing to Mrs. Pine.

"That? Oh..." Mama Roux trailed off a minute as she looked from Rex to the woman and back again. "That's one of... the demon's people. You remember. She tried to buy her way out with regular money."

"Do you know her story?" Marius asked.

"She came here a bit ago. Can't remember which day.

Sold her soul to Rex," Mama Roux said quietly. "You know how that goes."

"Why didn't you stop her?"

"This place is neutral. I can't be policin' what folks want to do. It's one reason we get help from the High Mystics."

"But what if *she* needs help?" Marius asked.

His eyes locked onto the woman pacing outside. It was not the angry Mrs. Pine he was used to. Not the thunderously stomping, ruler-slapping woman he knew. This woman was bent over with fear. She seemed even more desperate than she had at school, and now it was coupled with absolute terror.

"Child, I did try to speak to her. She made a bargain. She wanted her kids to be well," Mama Roux said with a heavy breath. "She sold her soul because one of them was really sick. The doctors plum gave up on them. Now she's here to pay up on her debt."

"Are her kids going to be okay?"

"I hope so, petit. That's the thing with crossroad demons. They feed on people's desperation, but they are in charge of the contracts. They know dat fine print. If he takes her soul, he has to cure her child. But they're all trouble. They will twist whatever needs twistin' to get you to pay up early or make it harder on you. Your mama found that out the hard way."

A hot, gurgling anger rose inside Marius. It erupted so steadily, it lifted him from his seat. The world turned into shades of black and red. He was walking toward the smirking demon before he even realized his legs were moving.

"It's not the same one, son. He wasn't the one who came for me."

"It doesn't matter, Mom. This is wrong," Marius said.

"This is nothing but trouble."

"I don't care."

He covered the distance in seconds. It felt like only a few steps but could have been as many as fifty. For some reason time and place stopped making sense.

"Let her go," Marius said in a low growl.

"What have we here? The baby hunter?" Rex asked, turning to face Marius.

"Let that woman go. Release her from her contract."

"Why, in all of the fires of Hell, would I do that?" Rex asked, sounding more amused than anything else.

"Because her kid was sick. She shouldn't have to lose her soul for that."

"How sweet you are, Marius Grey. Not the good sweet, mind you. No, I think you are more like the deep sweet that gives a person a cavity. Go away from me, cavity boy," Rex said, shooing Marius away with a dismissive hand gesture.

Marius stared at the demon and then back outside. Mrs. Pine had made it to the dining room door. Her hand trembled as she reached for the handle. Fresh tears poured down her cheeks.

He thought about his mother. He pictured her having to make that deal. Did she tremble and cry? Did she beg for her life? Or did the demon just throw her car off the road before she knew the difference?

In that moment, he did not see the teacher who constantly yelled at him. He saw a mom. A frightened mother who had kids who would never see her again.

"I'll pay her debt," Marius said.

"That's cute, boy. With what?" Rex said, meeting his gaze. "I don't accept bottle caps or jellybeans or whatever human children deal in."

"Be careful, Marius. Staring into a demon's eyes is like waltzing into red-hot madness. Don't spend too long doing it, or you'll lose yourself."

It was wholly disconcerting looking into Rex's eyes. Marius saw what his mother meant. Staring at the demon elicited strange sensations. He could see fire, smell sulfur, and taste brimstone in the back of his throat. Rex had not been his mother's tormentor, but Marius figured it must be the same with all crossroad demons. What a horrible sight to get used to.

Marius gathered his courage and reached into his pocket. There sat the hundred-Mystic coin. It felt cool in his fingers. Thinking back on the last week, Marius could not say why he had not deposited the coin with the others in his safe. He'd thought about it often while weeding the graveyard or chatting with Rhiannon. Something had always come up, and he had not followed through. Now he wondered if this was the reason.

With a renewed confidence, Marius slapped the Mystic coin down on the table. Rex actually looked surprised. It was hard to shock a demon, but Rex's eyebrows rose almost to his hairline. A crude smile spread on his face as he picked up the coin and examined it.

"Where did you get this, baby hunter? Following in your mother's footsteps?"

"It doesn't matter. Will this pay her debt?" Marius asked.

"Yes, this will do," Rex said. His words came out smooth and slithering. "Are you sure, baby hunter? What is this woman to you?"

"Just take it and let her go," Marius said.

His voice was dark and full of gravel. Marius barely recognized it.

Rex managed to smile even larger, as though all this life-and-death talk was incredibly amusing. It was not until that moment that Marius noticed the silence in the dining room. Most conversation had ceased. Even the humans who knew nothing of the other world stopped talking.

"All right, young Marius. Her debt is paid in full. She may keep her soul," Rex said. "Pleasure doing business with you. Give me a call if you ever want to follow in your mother's *other* footsteps."

The demon pocketed the Mystic coin. With a wave of his

hand, the door opened, inviting Mrs. Pine inside the building. She came in with a set jaw and clenched fists by her side.

Marius veered away from the demon and stormed back over to his table. He hid his face behind one of Mama Roux's laminated menus that seemed to always be sticky for some reason. His teacher did not notice him.

"I . . . I'm here," she said down to the demon.

"It appears your trip here was unnecessary," he said smoothly.

"What . . . what do you mean?"

"Your debt has been paid."

Her entire body relaxed, and some of the blood returned to her face.

"It has? How? Who paid it?"

Rex cast a quick glance in Marius's direction. He ducked farther behind the menu. Mrs. Pine was still gaping at the demon, unaware Marius was so close by. Rex opened his mouth to say more but was quickly cut off by Mama Roux.

"Hello, cher. Can I get you somethin' to eat?" she asked Mrs. Pine. "You look right starved. A good breeze might blow you over."

"I . . . uh, no thank you. I'm not here to eat."

"Then what are you here for?" Mama Roux asked. She stared deep into Mrs. Pine's eyes, enveloping all of the teacher's attention. "If you ain't here for food, maybe you best run on home and take care of that sweet babe of yours. Some questions are best left unasked in this sort of place."

"Yes," she said through numb lips. "I think I will do that."

Mrs. Pine turned on her heel and hurried out of the restaurant. Marius watched her disappear as the door shut between them. The next thing he saw was Mama Roux standing over his table. There was no hiding from her.

"Marius Grey, where on earth did you get dat much money?" she asked, wringing her hands together.

He did not answer her. There was too much anger in him. Any words that came out would be mean, and Mama Roux did not deserve that. Marius merely shook his head.

"I expect an explanation, child," she said.

"I will. Not today," he said through gritted teeth. "Please, Mama Roux. Not today."

Marius prepared for something more. Badgering, yelling, threats to withhold food. He braced for it by ducking his head and lacing his fingers in his hair.

To his utter surprise, that did not happen. Several long breaths passed between them while the great woman decided what to do. In the end, Mama Roux nodded to him and patted his shoulder.

"I expect you to tell me soon."

"I will," he said, still unable to look her in the eye.

"You're a good boy, Marius Grey."

She left him there without another word.

CHAPTER TWENTY-ONE

"Why did you give up your money?" Rhiannon asked in a flat tone. She held on to the edge of the boat, listening to his story. "You don't even like her."

"That's not the point. She was going to get sent to Hell."

"She made the deal, right? She knew . . ."

"It doesn't matter!" Marius shouted.

Rhiannon flinched a little, bobbing her head beneath the surface of the water. When she returned, she appeared more annoyed than frightened. Marius sighed deeply and counted backward from ten.

"I'm sorry," he said.

"It's not my fault," she said. A small pout formed on her face.

"I know it's not."

"You humans are so weird sometimes. Why would you help someone you don't like? With us, it's simple. You either love someone or you eat someone. There's not all this weird other stuff."

"Weird other stuff?" he asked.

"Yeah, this in-between stuff. It's dumb."

"I just . . . I just needed to help her, but that was a lot of money. At this rate, I'm never going to save enough in time. The two-year mark is almost up. I've got five days."

"How much do you need?"

"One hundred and fifty now," he said, sounding deflated. "I've been saving since she died."

"Well, there's always the rougarou. Didn't Papa Harold say he had a bounty for one in the swamp?"

"Yes, that would get me where I need. A rougarou would be worth way more than a boo hag. Maybe more than twenty boogeymen."

Marius shivered inwardly. Even though the evening was warm and humid, he felt cold all over. Old tales of mutilated hunters drifted into his mind. Nothing left to identify a body except some teeth and animal scat. His mother scared him properly telling those stories when he was young.

Rougarous were beasts of the swamp. Land and water animals. The accounts from survivors varied, but a few things lined up. A rougarou had a wolf's head and claws, and sometimes the tail and tough hide of an alligator. It was often described as werewolf-like, huge and terrifying. Of course, werewolves were ridiculously made up things, as were vampires. The silly musings of humans, but rougarous definitely played a part in the werewolf legends.

The thought of going after a rougarou made Marius break out into a cold sweat. It was wholly disconcerting to shiver and sweat at the same time. He was so stuck in his own thoughts that he did not hear Rhiannon speaking until she touched his hand.

"Marius, are you listening?" she said, staring into his eyes.

"Sorry, I was miles away."

"But you didn't leave," she said.

"It's a human saying. It means I was thinking too hard . . . about the rougarou."

"Are you sure you want to hunt it? I mean, you can go back to hunting boogeymen and small stuff. It's safer," she said.

"Rhia, I've been hunting small stuff for two years, and I'm still so far away from what I need. It will take me another two years to get there. I think I have to do this."

"You sure?" she asked with a skeptical raise of one eyebrow.

"I need to go after the rougarou to get the money in one swoop. I just don't know how to find it."

"I think I may be able to help with that," she said. "I know a fifolet family that lives nearby. A whole clan of them, really. I bet if you get them to help, they could lead you to the rougarou."

"Oh, Rhia, I know better than to follow a fifolet. They

love to hang around fishing holes and lead fishermen astray. That's all they do. Get people lost. How could they possibly help us?"

"If you offer them a present, they will take you where you want to go," she said.

"Like what? I can't afford to lose any more money."

"They don't want money. They love virgin water. You know, water that hasn't touched the earth yet or any pipes."

"But I don't have any virgin water. It hasn't rained in weeks, so I haven't collected any," Marius said.

"Well, I bet you know someone who does," Rhia said, raising her eyebrows.

"Oh no. No, I can't," Marius said.

"You know she has to have some," Rhia said.

"Madame Millet doesn't part with her ingredients for anything. She won't sell them or barter for them. Everyone knows that," Marius said.

Rhiannon lowered her head into the water. She still held on with her sharp fingernails, but her face submerged to her nose. When she gazed up at Marius with her large eyes, she looked almost innocent. Rhiannon popped her head up just enough to speak.

"You could steal the virgin water," Rhiannon said.

She managed to pull off a sheepish smile when she spoke.

"How on earth would I do that? The house is always full of people. Her personal storeroom is in the parlor under lock and key. Only Madame Millet has a copy. Not to mention, Mildred stalks that place like it's her own personal castle."

"I can make you a key," Rhiannon said.

"You can? How?"

The mermaid held out her arm with her delicate wrist pointing upward. Rhiannon concentrated on her skin. He could not tell what she was trying to do. Marius moved in closer to get a better look, but she held up a finger to stop him.

"Not too close," she said.

"Why?"

As soon as he asked, a long spike shot out from Rhiannon's wrist. It protruded about six inches from the palm of her hand. Marius nearly jumped overboard. He did not know mermaids had barbs inside their arms. It stuck out like a tiny spear.

"It's not going to bite, silly human," Rhiannon said, giggling to herself. "Get your knife."

Marius did as instructed. He pulled out his fillet knife and inspected the spike. It was the color of her sharp fingernails. Black at the tip and bone colored beneath. He stuck out a finger and pressed the spot where her skin met the barb. He felt it under her flesh all the way down into her skeleton.

"It's good for catching fish," she said, answering his unasked question. "It's also good for unlocking things. You'd be surprised how many doors we need to unlock."

Visions of sunken treasure chests and abandoned ship-wrecks filled his head, but he did not have the headspace to go there with her at that moment. He made a mental note to ask her about it later.

"So, I can use this to open her door?" Marius asked.

"Yes. Just cut off the tip of it with your knife. You can use it to open her door. These open just about any lock."

"But I don't want to hurt you," he said.

"It doesn't hurt. Like clipping a fingernail. It grows back."

"You sure I won't hurt you?"

"Just cut from underneath like this," Rhiannon said, placing the blade's edge underneath the barb and away from her skin.

A few quick saws, and Marius was the proud owner of a three-inch mermaid barb. Nature's skeleton key. Another secret most monster hunters did not know.

"Now all I need is a way to sneak into her parlor with-out her in it," he said.

"You would need help. A distraction," she said.

"Too bad you can't help me there," he said.

Rhiannon furrowed her brow as she concentrated. Mar-ius had gone through great lengths to keep the mermaid off everyone's radar. She could not go near the shore.

"What about a ghost?" she asked.

"Ghosts can't leave during the day. This would need to be a day job. Nighttime is when Madame Millet hosts par-ties and reads tarot. That won't work."

"Well, I'm out of ideas. You need a daytime friend that can go with you."

Marius thought about daytime friends. His stomach sank when he realized he did not really have any. Antoine had been a possibility, but after that handshake, that idea was out the window.

There was a slight giggle on the wind. It sounded like someone stifling a laugh. When he looked around, he spotted Hugo peeping from behind a tree. He was spying on them. As soon as Marius got a glimpse of Hugo, the lutin vanished.

A smile pulled at the corners of Marius's mouth. Lutins were able to go out during the day if there was a cemetery person to escort them. The one thing lutins loved the most was mischief. Marius had found his perfect distraction.

"Not all ghosts have to wait for nighttime."

CHAPTER TWENTY-TWO

The next day, Marius ditched school entirely. Instead, he found himself at the Habada-Chérie, face-to-face with Papa Harold. For some reason, he looked even worse in the daytime. There were no windows in the place to let in the sunlight, but still, it was true.

"I'm here about the rougarou," Marius said with a rich old air.

"Is that so? Well then, follow me," he said with a bow.

The shopkeeper led the monster hunter back to his room. Marius took his usual seat across from Papa Harold. He smelled the incense, but it was fainter than usual, like it was yesterday's scent. Sandalwood lingered in the pillows and curtains from days past. The Habada-Chérie must not get visitors this early in the day.

Papa Harold sat in his seat with a tired *whoosh* of air and produced his ledger. Marius pulled his book from his pocket and placed it on the table. He flipped through the pages of monsters past in an effort not to give away his nervousness.

There were poltergeists and boogeymen, even a few candy ladies. One time, he had bagged a grunch while rowing through his swamp. Grunches were goat-headed, apelike monsters who sucked their victims dry of blood. Marius had stumbled upon the creature and screamed the incantation purely from reflex.

Each page held the name and illustration of another creature captured. Another fiend taken from the world who could never hurt anyone ever again. It was a little odd to come across the page that read *Mermaid*. Just a blank page with no illustration. He had never turned in that bounty, of course. Rhiannon's face would never grace his book.

All thoughts of Rhiannon went out the window when he got to the boo hag's page. Her ghastly face and skeletal body seemed to scream at him from inside her illustration. According to this, her name had been Edelmira. Marius shivered at the memory and turned the page.

Papa Harold ripped a new sheet of paper from his ledger and placed it delicately on the blank page. As soon as he did, the blank page shimmered. The word *Rougarou* magically wrote itself in black ink across the top.

That was it. No going back now. The rougarou was his bounty.

"What info do you have on him?" Marius said, looking up at the grizzled shopkeeper.

"Well, oddly enough, he's been spotted in the swampland near you. You're off Bayou Rigolettes, aren't you?"

"Yes, but that doesn't narrow it down much. That's a big bayou and there's miles of connected swampland," Marius said.

"Unfortunately, most of my information has been from the hobbs showing up at my door wanting beer. Normally, I can rely on the gargoyles, but they generally don't go out into the swamps. They're not comfortable flying too far away from churches. Hobbs are good spies but only when they're sober, and none of them have been sober."

Hobbs closely resembled those garden gnome statues in clothes and size. While gnome statues were cute and humanlike, hobbs looked more like bats. They had large ears and turned-up noses. Their eyes were way too far apart from each other to be appealing.

They carried pencils and chalk everywhere because they loved to draw on everything. Regular humans did not realize that half of the time they walked over those sidewalk chalk drawings, they were trampling on the work of a hobb. It was normally harmless unless they were drunk. That was when the drawings got lewd.

"So somewhere near me in the swamplands of Bayou Rigolettes is as good as you can give me?" Marius asked.

"Everything I know is now in your book. It's not much,

but you are a resourceful hunter. I've seen you capture a monster going on less than that. Hell, that candy lady . . ."

"Boo hag," Marius corrected.

"Yes, the boo hag. You found her primarily on your own wiles. You can do this," Papa Harold said.

"I will do my best," Marius said.

He looked down into his book and sighed when he read *Rougarou* again. An ominous air filled the room around that word. They were among the most dangerous monsters in the South. Fiercer than an alligator, and more devious than any boo hag.

Marius ran his finger along the edge of his book. The act calmed him by a degree. There was a kinship between a monster hunter and his book. They were extensions of each other. Marius often found himself thinking of the book as alive.

As if reading his thoughts, the edge of the book shuddered under his finger. Marius grabbed the volume and shoved it into his inside pocket.

"There's no shame in backing down," Papa Harold said, suddenly standing behind him. Marius jumped when he placed a warm hand on his shoulder. "If you give up, I wouldn't tell a soul. I worry about you and this bounty, young Mister Grey. When I offered, I didn't really think you would take it."

"I'm going to get him. I will collect the rougarou and bring him back here," Marius said with determination.

He even nodded with the last words as if to accent his point.

"Very well, child. Good luck to you. Just remember, no bounty is worth your life."

Marius left the shop without another word. He barely waved farewell to Papa Harold. It was hard to speak when your teeth were clenched, and the monster hunter started shaking before he rounded the corner.

CHAPTER TWENTY-THREE

The day of the heist was all too pleasant. Sunshine streamed down on the inhabitants of New Orleans without a cloud in the sky. A gentle breeze crept through the trees, keeping the air from sitting stagnant in place. Everything seemed saturated with color. The blue sky, the green grass. Marius might have whistled, it was so pleasant. Too bad he was shaking in his boots from nervousness.

"If you must engage in dirty work, stick to the daylight hours. There are far too many things that can watch you at night."

"I know, Mom. Only people can watch you during the day, and they won't notice us anyway," Marius said, repeating one of his mother's many lessons in a bored tone.

"Well, you remembered it, didn't you? You may think they're stupid, but they stuck."

"Yeah, yeah. You're right . . . again," Marius said.

"Who are you talking to?" Hugo whispered to Marius.

"No one, really. Just . . . myself."

Marius approached Madame Millet's house, trying to act aloof and calm. Hugo followed behind him, invisible to everyone. Well, everyone except the polydactyl cats. Normally, they lounged about the expansive porch, ignoring everyone and soaking up the sun. Now they stood on high alert, crouching behind trees and rocking chairs. Their eyes were wide and dark with their dilated pupils.

"Best you go inside," Marius whispered to Hugo. "Don't start messing with stuff until I say the word *beignets*."

"Okay, gotcha," Hugo said quietly.

Marius felt a slight whoosh of air, and the lutin was gone. One of the cats growled in that high-pitched way cats do as he walked up the steps. Marius hissed at the cat. Well, it was his best imitation of a cat's hiss. It worked. The cats fluffed up and scampered away.

His grand hopes for a quick mission were dashed outright when he knocked on the door and Mildred answered. She wore a purple dress, all decorated in baubles and tulle. Dark eyeliner and glitter mascara embellished her deep-set eyes. She did not look particularly happy to be made up.

"What do you want?" she snapped. "There's no school on Saturdays."

"You look like a French clown doll brought to life."

"I ought to slap you, Marius Grey!"

"Don't get any glitter on me," he said, shielding his eyes with a mocking smile.

Mildred popped him a good one on his arm. He heard

a tinkling and saw two purple-gemmed fingernails fall on the ground. They had snapped off Mildred's hand. He picked them up and handed them back with a wide grin.

"Your nails, milady," he said, bowing to her.

Mildred snatched the nails from his hand. Her face was red with embarrassment.

"What do you want, orphan?" she snapped.

"I need to speak with your maman," he said.

"She is getting ready for a party. Can't you hear it?" Mildred said pointedly. The sounds of caterers and musicians bustled about. "Besides, you're not dressed right in that old raggedy coat of yours."

"Looks like you are underdressed too with those raggedy hands. Just tell her I'm here, Mildred. It's been a long day."

She rolled her eyes and slammed the door in his face. Marius waited on the porch. Part of him hoped Mildred would forget or not tell her mother on purpose. If that happened, he had a chance of knocking again and getting someone else who might actually help him. When the door creaked back open, it was Madame Millet on the other side.

"Mister Grey. What are you doing here?"

"I needed to ask you something important."

"Oh?"

"Can I go to your office? I'd like to talk alone."

"Sure," Madame Millet said, opening the door wider. "I meant what I said, Marius. My door is always open."

A sharp pang of guilt stung him right in the ribs. He ignored it and continued. In for a penny, in for a pound.

Passing through the incantation on her office door, Marius made a note to himself not to leave in anger. *All who come are welcome. All who leave in anger are fools.* He just really hoped leaving with stolen goods was far enough away from leaving in anger to keep him from getting cursed.

"Now, what is this all about?" Madame Millet said.

She closed the door behind her and placed a firm hand on his shoulder. It was warm and comforting. Guilt stabbed him a few more times.

"I . . . I've just been worried about Mrs. Pine," he said.

It was not a complete lie. He had been worried about the math teacher.

"Oh, isn't that nice of you. I'm glad you are softening to her. And to answer your question, yes, she seems to be better. She gained a little weight back, which is good. You could knock her over with a feather before."

"Yeah, I was just thinking she could use some food. I actually thought about bringing beignets one morning for everyone," he said.

Madame Millet smiled so brightly, it hurt Marius's heart. He decided that if he lived through all of this, he would make good on his promise. After all, who did not like Cajun donuts?

Their conversation was cut short by a crashing sound on the other side of the door. Marius heard the twins dash by in a fit of giggles. Two more bangs and another crash. She released Marius's shoulder in a hurry. Madame Millet threw open the door to complete and utter chaos.

"What in blue blazes!" she shouted.

Picture frames rocked this way and that on the wall. A series of colored balls bounced up and down the stairs completely on their own. Silverware clattered in the kitchen on overturned pots and pans. Marcel and Mina dashed through the hall laughing hysterically and smashing vases. A disembodied boy's laugh echoed through the house.

Hugo had done his job.

"How did we get a poltergeist? Mina, Marcel, get back here! Stop smashing that. Get my salt. Where is your sister!"

Madame Millet stormed into the chaos, leaving Marius alone in the parlor. Now was his chance. He slipped behind her chair and through her blue velvet curtain. The door was narrow, more so than most doors. The ancient doorknob had the skull with the three Xs carved on top of it and a keyhole just below. Marius pulled Rhiannon's barb from his outer pocket and stuck it in the lock.

Much to his delight, the lock clicked immediately, but when he tried to turn his makeshift key, it refused to budge. He tried to jiggle and force it, but the bolt refused to turn over. Marius groaned inwardly.

Of course, the lock was charmed, he thought. Rhiannon's barb might open regularly locked doors, but Madame Millet put a spell on her lock as extra protection. He racked his brain, trying to think of something that dissolved lock spells. If only he paid more attention in class.

"Sage smoke. It cleanses most charms."

"I don't know if I have any," Marius whispered, digging in his many pockets.

Luckily, he found a small bundle hidden under a package of jasmine. He pulled it out and inspected the squashed bundle. It was a collection of dried sage leaves with braided thread winding tightly around it. There was only about two inches left, but he would have to make it work.

He lit the end of the sage with a match, hoping no one would smell the smoke. In the distance, there was the sound of something breaking, followed by giddy screams. A little sage smoke would probably not be noticed.

When an orange ember bloomed in the center, he slowly blew out the flame. Gray smoke snaked upward, filling his nose with burning herbs. Marius held the bundle to the lock and blew the vapor into the keyhole. When he turned the mermaid barb, it rotated easily. The lock clicked.

Marius blew out a sigh of relief as he smudged out the burning sage on the bottom of his shoe. If poachers knew that a little sage and a mermaid barb could open most doors, Rhiannon's kind would be massacred by the hundreds. Marius shuddered at the thought, turned the knob, and entered the secret room.

Madame Millet was a hoarder of ingredients. Shelf after

shelf, row after row, was stacked high with valuable magics. Not even the Habada-Chérie could boast such a collection. In fact, they probably did not have even a quarter of this storeroom's wealth.

Marius oscillated between feeling extreme guilt for intruding on Madame Millet's privacy and feeling impressed by her collection. It must have taken ages to build it up. There was no time to stare in wonder. Who knew how long Hugo could keep up the distraction with Madame Millet trying to exorcize him.

Stone obelisks, fossilized bird eggs, petrified wood masks, and opaline geodes lined the walls. A series of curio cabinets held embalmed pig fetuses, mummified cats, the remains of a three-headed puppy. He found a large typesetter's case nailed vertically in the wall. A number of different hourglasses and timepieces filled the small compartments along with a pristine mummified seahorse with a tiny unicorn's horn.

He stopped for a hot minute and noticed something he had not expected to find. Behind a glass cabinet stood a set of scales that he recognized. They were the same kind of scales Papa Harold had. They had no other purpose than to weigh monster books.

Madame Millet processed monsters, or at least, she used to. Marius had a hard time wrapping his mind around that. She talked so much about how dangerous it was, but she owned a set of scales.

He decided to shake that off and continue on his hunt. It was something to ponder later.

Another cabinet held her assortment of mandrake roots. They took the form of tiny people with leaves sprouting from their heads, each one in their own little jar. Some were male and some female. The oldest were able to move in their glass prisons while the babies merely slept. Marius ran a finger over one of the larger jars and the adult mandrake swiveled around, trying to break free.

"Careful. Don't let it loose. Nothing is worse than pulling a mandrake's roots from underneath your skin. They can dig in like ticks in seconds."

"I wasn't going to let it loose, Mom," Marius whispered.

"Well, stop dillydallying. That wicked little girl is around here somewhere. If you get caught . . ."

"I'm not dillydallying! I don't know where she keeps her virgin water."

"I don't like this plan. It's all a bad idea. Why would you listen to that mermaid? She's just as much of a monster as the rougarou."

"That's it. I've had it," Marius said in a harder whisper. "Rhia is my friend. You left me all alone! Say one more bad thing about her, and I will never talk to you again."

He whipped around the room as though he might get a glimpse of her. It was a foolish act. The truth was he never knew if the voice he heard was his mother's or not. He spoke to it, he argued with it, but there was no way to tell if it was really her. It could just as easily be his own mind filling in the space where she would have been. After all, she never said anything he did not already know.

He thought briefly about apologizing, just in case it was his mother's voice all along. *What good would it do?* he thought. What could anyone really say after that? Besides, he had to locate the virgin water quickly before he was found out.

Marius found a section of the room reserved for more mundane items. Here was the brick dust, salt, rosemary, and eucalyptus. The chicken feet, beads, and rosaries. Just behind the tray of tiger's eye eggs sat several jars of virgin water. Marius grabbed one and hurried out of the forbidden room, locking the door behind him.

When he threw back the velvet curtain, he came face-to-face with Mildred Millet. He might have jumped out of his skin, but fear froze him solidly in place. There was a heartbeat's worth of time where he scanned the parlor for anyone else. No one but Mildred, not that it mattered. She was enough.

CHAPTER TWENTY-FOUR

"I've got you now, Mary. I caught you stealing, and you are going to pay. Vengeful Faery, blood and bone. Expel this criminal from our home!" Mildred shouted, throwing a palmful of glittery faery dust in Marius's face.

All at once, the floor flew out from beneath Marius's feet, and he shot backward. A great burst of wind whipped past his ears. When his back hit the ground, he was no longer in Madame Millet's parlor. He was outside. Mildred's spell had transported him clear out of the house.

The sun blinded him, and he put up his hand to block it. Everything was so disconcerting. He blinked hard to get his bearings. He was on the front lawn. The polydactyl cats were hissing and growling around him. When he laid eyes on the front door, he spotted Mildred exiting the house and walking down the stairs. She held the jar of virgin water in her hand.

He did not know when she'd grabbed it. Perhaps just

before her spell propelled him from the house. Either way, she held it out like it was a sacred artifact.

"I am going to enjoy calling Maman out here. I'm going to tell her that you were stealing from her," Mildred said with a smug grin.

"Please, Mildred, don't say anything," Marius said, getting to his feet. "I'll go. I'll leave right now."

His innards shuddered at being found out. He looked this way and that to see if anyone else saw them in the yard. Luckily, there was no one but Mildred. Marius could run if she let him.

"No way, Mary. I've been looking for a good reason to get rid of you. Maman likes you for some stupid reason, but she won't any longer if she sees this," Mildred said, pointing to the virgin water. "She hates thieves."

"Please, don't. I have to get this bounty. I need that virgin water to do it."

"What good is virgin water to fighting a monster? I can exorcise a poltergeist in my sleep without this stuff."

"It's not a poltergeist," he said.

"Then what?" Mildred asked, rolling her eyes. "A boogeyman?"

"It's a rougarou!"

Mildred's mouth dropped. It was like he'd thrown stunning oil in her face. It took her a few seconds to recover her voice.

"Are you crazy? You can't get one of those. It'll kill you."

"I have to TRY!"

"All this to get a stinking rougarou. To what? Prove what a big hunter you are?" she asked in a mocking tone.

"It's not that," he said. "I need the water to track the monster. I can't collect the bounty without it."

Red heat lit the area behind his eyes. He was furious, but he would not let it show. Mildred was holding all the cards. If he broke and lashed out at her, it would be done. One call to her mother, and this would all be over. He was so frustrated he was about to scream.

"No one has virgin water. Everything's been dry for two months. And your mother doesn't sell or barter."

"Not. My. Problem," she said pointedly. Mildred turned on her heel toward the house. There was still a good deal of shouting and breaking glass inside. Mildred put a hand to her mouth and shouted, "Maman! I have something to tell you!"

"Please!" Marius exclaimed, grabbing Mildred's shoulder. She snapped around and threw his hand off her. "If you could bring your dad back, wouldn't you? Wouldn't you do anything, even stealing, if it brought him back to life?"

Mildred's face fell. Whatever she thought Marius was going to say, it obviously was not that. She gaped at the monster hunter, looking utterly confused. When the understanding hit her, it hit her like a slap in the face. Her words came out quiet and careful.

172

"That's why you're doing all this? You are trying to bring her back? Marius, she made that deal with the crossroad demon. She's gone. There's nothing you can do."

"I have to try. I can't leave her in Hell. I just can't. If there's a chance, I have to take it," he said, desperate tears falling down his face.

He felt small and stupid and alone. Marius wanted to be anywhere else but here. He was so tired of being strong. Living life as an orphaned twelve-year-old had left him hollowed out inside. Cemetery boy or not, he was tired of being lonely. There was no one to cook for him or hold him or tuck him into bed. No mother to hug him. Not ever again if he did not get that water.

Any other day, Mildred would find it hilarious to watch Marius Grey cry in front of her. That would be a red-letter occasion. She would fix herself popcorn and laugh at his whimpering. Marius guessed that was probably in her top five fantasies.

Now Mildred watched Marius fall to his knees in front of her. He sat cross-legged in the yard and put his head in his hands. He sniffled and dried his eyes with the back of his oversized coat sleeve.

Marius could not even meet her eyes. He was giving up. He was bested. It was over.

"Go ahead," he said, sounding deflated. "Go tell your maman. You're right. This would probably get me killed anyway. Turn me in. I deserve it."

Somewhere in the background, they heard shuffling noises from the house. The twins giddily ran past the opened door squealing like piglets. Madame Millet was hot on their heels, scolding as she ran.

"Get back here, the both of you!" she yelled. Then she turned to look outside. "Mildred, what were you saying? Why are you two out in the yard? Is something wrong?"

Marius took a deep breath and exhaled it into his hands. He waited for the inevitable. Any second now Mildred would raise her screechy voice and turn him in. Several decent lies flashed through his mind, but none that Madame Millet would buy. Especially not with Mildred telling her side of the story.

He was doomed.

"Nothing's wrong, Maman," Mildred yelled back over her shoulder. "Marius was just leaving. He forgot something is all."

Marius's head snapped up, and he met her gaze. It was stony and solid. She was sure of her words. It did not mean she liked him. No, there was still a heavy dose of hatred in those eyes. For some reason though, she was letting him go.

"Oh, okay. No fighting, you two," Madame Millet said before she ran back into the house.

Marius stood up and dusted off his pants with his hands. He did not break eye contact with Mildred. This truce felt so flimsy, like wet cardboard. He feared looking away would break whatever spell this was between them.

"Here," she said as she handed him the jar of virgin water. "Take it. Never tell anybody I was nice to you."

"Why are you? Why didn't you turn me in?" he asked.

Mildred made a hand motion toward the house.

"Because I wanted to bring Daddy back, but she wouldn't let me try. She wouldn't let anyone try. We did the spell to call his soul back when we found him, but it didn't work. He had been gone too long. Maman had the resurrection spell but wouldn't use it. Said it was too dangerous. I still don't think you can bring your mother back, but I don't want to be the one who told you that you can't try."

"I don't know what to say," Marius said.

He stuck out his hand for a shake. Instantly, he regretted it. It was an awkward motion between two people who had never shaken hands. She took one look at it and batted his hand away in disgust.

"Ewww, don't be weird. Just get your lutin out of here before he ruins the whole house," Mildred said with a scowl.

And just like that, Mildred Millet flipped her braids in Marius's face and left him all alone on the front lawn. Her moment of acting like a decent human being had been brief, but it happened. Had he not witnessed it for himself, Marius would never have believed such a thing could be possible.

CHAPTER
TWENTY-FIVE

Getting ready for the hunt was nerve-racking. Even though he had sworn Hugo to secrecy about their little adventure to Madame Millet's, Marius was nervous the lutin would blab to the other ghosts.

Despite all of Rhiannon's warnings against waiting too long, he took the ghosts to dinner the night the big hunt was going to take place. He needed food in his belly, and dinner always placated the cemetery inhabitants. Happy ghosts meant fewer questions.

After he escorted his ghosts back home, he made for his boat with an uneasy stomach. Normally, a fried basket of fish tasted better than anything in the world, but not tonight. His gut rumbled with his nerves. He stopped rowing several times on the way out because he thought he might throw up his recently consumed dinner.

"You can always turn back, my boy. I'm not worth all this."

"No. I'm getting you back."

"Be careful."

He did not need to toss the jasmine to let Rhiannon know he was there. She was waiting for him in their usual place. Her head bobbed out of the water, and she latched on to the boat with her hands.

Marius looked into her eyes and saw fear there. It was disconcerting because Rhiannon never looked afraid. Even when he first tried to collect her bounty, she was more curious than fearful. It was one reason he stopped to talk to her rather than cast his spell right away. He would always be thankful he did.

"Are you all right?" he asked her.

"I'm not hungry," Rhiannon said.

"I'm not sure what that means."

"I'm *always* hungry. I eat all the time. Constantly. Even when I'm full, I'm still kind of hungry," she said.

"I'm not following, Rhia."

"This is the first time I'm not hungry."

"I feel the same. It means we are afraid."

"I don't like it," Rhiannon said.

"Me neither," Marius said. "We should probably get going."

The plan was for Marius to row the boat, and Rhiannon would pull him to the place where the fifolets congregated at night. That was the next step, rowing and pulling. They both knew it, yet neither of them moved an inch. They just stared at each other, waiting for someone to make the first move.

"Why is she not one of your ghosts?" Rhiannon asked.

It was one of the last things he expected her to say. Well, maybe not. The last thing he expected her to say would be something along the lines of, "Let's go for a waltz on dry land." This, however, was not far off.

"Do you mean my mother? She can't . . . be a ghost."

"Why not? That's what you humans do, right?" she asked.

"Yes, when the timing and situation is right. But not my mom."

"Why not her? Why doesn't she go to dinner with you and the others in your cemetery?"

"She made a deal with a demon two years ago. Her soul if he would find my dad. The demon reneged on the contract, said my dad was unfindable. My mom backed out of the deal since he didn't hold up his end of the bargain. The demon found some kind of loophole and made my mom crash her car. She died, and he got her soul. At least, that's what I was told."

"But why is she not a ghost?"

"She went to Hell," Marius said, wincing at the last word. "People in Hell don't get ghosts. They don't get much of anything. Which is why I have to bring her back. I can't leave my mom to suffer there."

Rhiannon took in his words and bobbed her head just enough to be noticeable. It was always hard to read the mermaid. If Marius were to guess, he would call it a nod of conclusion. Resolution. It was a decisive gesture, one of action. She still looked afraid, but she took the rope tethered

178

to the boat and dove into the water. Marius took the oars and helped her along.

Time passed. It did not move fast or slow. Perhaps when there was no watch to read and no clock to measure hours, the world ticked along this way. A vacuum of seconds. The journey could take hours or minutes, and no one would have known the difference.

Marius breathed in and out; he moved the oars back and forth. But nothing marked his progress except a continual line of bayou and trees. The monotony had lulled him into such a trance, he almost missed the outcropping of stones that was their destination. Luckily, Rhiannon remembered and directed the little boat toward them.

They pulled up to the rocks and dropped anchor beside them. To any normal person, this would appear to be a normal series of flat stones. Large chunks of slate rested on top of each other in what could easily be confused for a random pattern.

The smallest stones were in the center, and the bigger ones grew out from there. They fanned upward making nature's equivalent of a small staircase. The installation was tiny. It was in the middle of nowhere, so humans would be hard-pressed to see it. Even if someone did, the half circle only reached up to a man's shinbone. Men rarely paid attention to things shorter than their knee.

"This is it," Rhiannon said. "This is the fifolet place. They congregate here."

"So, I should just put this water out here? In the middle?" Marius asked.

Rhiannon shrugged, but he took it as a good enough. He removed the jar of virgin water from his deepest coat pocket and placed it on the top center rock in the formation. He opened the lid carefully and moved away, settling back into the boat.

"Now what?" he asked.

"Ask them for help," she said, nudging him with her elbow.

He raised himself to a better posture and cleared his throat a few times. For some reason, he felt a little nervous. Marius swallowed back the jitters and addressed the unseen fifolet clan.

"I am Marius Grey," he said loudly. It was too loud and got a warning glare from Rhiannon. He began again but softer. "I am Marius Grey, and I need your help. I need to find the rougarou that lives in this swampland. I am offering the fifolets here virgin water as a payment."

Nothing happened. Not a bird moved. Not a frog croaked. The mosquitos still buzzed because not even a rougarou was able to stop those from tormenting everything in sight.

"What now?" he whispered.

"I don't know. I guess they will come out if they agree to your terms," Rhiannon said.

"And if they don't come out?"

"I guess we did all this for nothing," she said with a shrug.

They did not have to wait long. Slowly, cautiously, a few tiny green lights danced out from behind some cypress branches. Then a few more. Before long, two dozen fifolets bobbed their way through the air toward the jar of virgin water.

Marius had never seen one up close and never so many. If you caught sight of a fifolet, it was fleeting. You might play it off as a trick of the light. A flash in the corner of your eye. Now he could see they were lights, but also so much more than that.

They looked like tiny bubbles with tendrils that flowed out and sucked in with every dipping movement. It was like watching a whole family of jellyfish floating in the air. Each fifolet danced around the one next to it, making their paths forever varied. No wonder they found it so easy to draw humans away and get them lost.

They congregated near the open jar. Each one waited patiently as the next took a sip. It was a beautiful, tiny light show Marius had the pleasure to witness. Few ever did.

"I think you have your answer," Rhiannon said.

Her voice dipped low, and when Marius turned to face her, the mermaid's gaze fell to the water. She sank low enough to submerge her nose.

"This is good though, right?" he said. "It's what we wanted."

"It's what *you* wanted," she said. Rhiannon used her hands to raise herself up. She stared intently into Marius's eyes. "But you don't have to want it. We could go back."

"But, Rhia, we came all this way..."

His words were cut short. Rhiannon grabbed the back of his head with one hand and pressed her lips to his. All words left his mind. Everything left his mind. The rougarou, the mission, the cemetery. Marius forgot about it all. The world spun, so he shut his eyes against it. He floated in a space where he remembered nothing.

He existed in a void. No pain, no history, no thoughts beyond the here and now. Slowly, a beautiful light burned away the dark things. All that was left was a world of water. Floating endlessly with a pretty young mermaid. There was no danger to be seen.

"This is mermaid magic, Marius."

He recognized the voice but did not have a name for it yet. It was female to be sure but pulling the memories forth was like moving in molasses. Every step was exhausting. Was that his name? Was it Marius?

"They don't just sing and lure men to their deaths. Sometimes, they make them forget. That's what she's doing, son. Making you forget."

Son. That was right. If he was someone's son, that meant he had a mother and a father. He had a life and a purpose. What was it? There was a mission. He was here to do something important.

"Marius, wake up!"

Marius snapped his head back, ending the kiss with Rhiannon. He fell on his rear inside the belly of the boat, looking wildly up at the mermaid. Her lips were rosy pink, and her eyes flew wide. Everything came back to him like someone had thrown a bucket of cold water in his face.

"Why did you do that? Why were you trying to make me forget about this?" Marius asked.

He struggled to get to his feet. It was not easy to stand on a boat that small, but he felt like being taller than her at that moment. His face was flushed all over, hot and rosy.

"How did you break the spell?" Rhiannon asked, looking stunned.

"That's not the part you should be upset about! Why were you trying to bespell me into forgetting? Why did you . . . kiss me?"

The mermaid's eyebrows furrowed dramatically as she pulled herself straighter. Her mouth formed into a tight, angry line. Those aquamarine eyes of hers darkened into a forest green that almost appeared black in the moonlight.

"Because you are stupid. Humans are stupid. *This* is stupid. Going after a rougarou is stupid!"

"You helped me," he began, but she cut him off.

"Because we are friends. You are my only friend. I helped you, but I hoped this wouldn't happen. I thought maybe you wouldn't get the water, and then you did. I hoped the fifolets wouldn't show up, but they did. And now...now you are going to go, and it's so stupid!"

"Rhia, I have to..."

"No! You don't have to. Your mother is gone, and I don't want you to be gone too!"

Rhiannon slammed her hands into the top of the boat. Her barbs shot out, stabbing the wood with a loud *thwack*! Marius jumped back. He had to put both hands out to not fall over. The boat rocked a little this way and that. None of it seemed to spook the fifolets.

The mermaid tore her eyes from Marius to see she was pinned in place. When she took in the sight of her hands, her mouth fell open. She had just noticed her spikes came out. With a flexing of her muscle they retracted back into her arms. When she met Marius's gaze again, her eyes were back to normal. They filled with water in seconds.

"Wait, Rhia, it's okay," Marius said.

Rhiannon shook her head. Without another word, she dove into the water and disappeared beneath the blackness of the nighttime bayou. Marius stood in the boat, hoping in vain that she might surface. He waited because he did not want to do this alone. He could not stand leaving things this way. If she came back, everything would be fixed. All she had to do was swim back.

The night greeted him with nothing but the buzzing of mosquitos.

CHAPTER TWENTY-SIX

The fifolets seemed to have no agenda. They watched Marius and Rhiannon fight, and they were waiting still when he gave up on the mermaid. It took some doing for the monster hunter to sidestep the rock formation and join them. He was careful not to knock over the remaining water. They probably would not help him if he upset their home or their offering.

As he neared, the fifolets floated to his eyeline and drifted south. Marius had to wade in knee-deep water and pull himself through some moss to get to a shoreline he could travel. Being wary creatures of the air, the fifolets floated near enough for him to track but not close enough to touch.

The terrain varied as most of Louisiana does. Swampland and marshes emptied into bayous and tributaries. There was no rhyme or reason to the network of waterways. Mother nature did not build in grids, especially in the bayous. Luckily, there had been no rain for a while, giving Marius more dry land than he would normally have to maneuver.

The night was no longer young. He could tell that by the height of the moon. It was not a full moon, but it was full enough to see by. Had there been a cemetery nearby, his cemetery boy status would have given him the extra light he needed. Alas, there were no graves here. None that were marked, anyway.

"Don't think about dead people. And the light would only make you a target. Just keep moving and stay alert."

"What do I do, Mom? How do I win? I'm so afraid," he said.

He spoke quietly in short, shivering gasps of air. This far out in the swamp, there were no people noises. No cars driving, no laughing, no music, and certainly no conversations. When Marius spoke, his words sounded harsh and too loud.

"Your brick dust won't work. Salt is better. Remember, a rougarou isn't born. It's made."

"How is it made? How do I kill it?"

"Somewhere out here, a witch crafted it from the corpses of the fiercest creatures. Man, wolf, and gator. It is bound by enchanted thread. To break the creature, cut the thread."

"How will I find it?" Marius asked.

Just then, the fifolets reached a clearing in the swamp. The edge of the water ended in a crescent beach. It was made of dirt and peppered with stones. Beyond the beach was a mossy meadow, probably underwater during the rainier months. There was no tree cover, so the moon lit up the area.

The fifolets swarmed around one another in agitation before darting away in all directions. Each one flew in a different path. Their lights dimmed to nothing in the eerie night. Marius froze, trying to decide which one he was supposed to follow.

A deep, tremorous howl echoed into the swamp. The bayou water shivered underneath it. Birds twitched in the trees and flew away from the clearing. It was quite obvious why the fifolets left in a hurry. They had fulfilled their part. They brought Marius to the rougarou.

Marius suddenly found himself unable to take another step. In fact, he was fairly sure he forgot how to move in general. He heard the heavy panting of a huge creature just past the shore, but he had not spotted it yet.

"Run, Marius. You don't have to do this. Run away."

"No, I have to. I have to try," he whispered.

Saying that gave him a little courage that was not there before. He was here. No going back now. Marius found that he could, in fact, move. He ducked low and told himself that the creature had probably not seen him yet. If it had, Marius would already be dead. This gave him the small advantage of preparation.

Marius crouched as low as he was able, sneaking along the edge of the water. There were lots of reeds and tall grass that muffled his footsteps as he went. His first thought was to draw his salt circle next to the shore. His second thought was that was stupid because an alligator could ambush him. His third thought was that no alligator in its right mind would come close to a rougarou, so the first thought was probably a good plan.

For all Marius's planning and preparing, he was at a loss about how to go about this. Perhaps he and Rhiannon had been of like minds. Maybe he too never thought it would get this far. Something or someone was sure to stop him along the way. Some adult would step up and intervene. Madame Millet or Mama Roux, perhaps? They never did, so he was here now, and he had to figure it out.

Marius pulled out the salt flask from his coat pocket. With a shaking hand, he drew a large salt circle around himself. He nearly dropped the flask when the rougarou howled again. This time, it was closer, and a series of deep growls followed. The beast knew he was there.

He found the book in its usual spot in his inner pocket. Slowly, he removed it and flipped to the blank page with the word *Rougarou* written on the top. Marius tried hard to regulate his breaths, but it was no use. His heart pulsed inside his skull, rattling everything in his vision. When the rougarou moved into sight, Marius nearly lost his nerve.

It was at least seven feet tall, maybe more. The creature stood on two powerful legs with a spiked alligator tail behind it. Its torso was humanlike, but too large to be a man. More like a gorilla than anything else. The beast's arms hung long and low by its side with huge claws on each finger. The head was that of a wolf, but the fur on the face was stark white in contrast to the dark hair everywhere else.

The rougarou growled again and snapped its jaw three times at Marius. Something primal inside told him to run. Now. Run far away and never look back. Somehow, the reasonable side of his brain was working. It told him to be as still as possible. Running would lead him out of the circle. Out of the circle meant certain death. There was no outrunning a rougarou anyway.

With another terrible howl, the beast charged at Marius. It was impossibly fast and leaped toward him with claws out and fangs poised to bite. The rougarou hit an invisible barrier at the salt line. It knocked the beast to the ground, leaving it snorting and snarling at Marius.

The monster hunter was stunned, too much to hold the book like he ought. He dropped it to the ground while he tried to find his lost courage.

Up close, the creature was even more terrifying. There was a strange collaboration of textures on his body. Mostly fur and scales but also some human flesh. He searched the body to see where there might be a seam, anything to expose an enchanted thread, but he saw none. It appeared to be a whole being. Perhaps his mother's voice was wrong.

The rougarou growled again and threw itself against the salt barrier, but it did not give way. Marius retrieved the book from the ground and held it out to the beast snarling in front of him.

"Grab the arm, grab the crook. Stomp the ground until it's shook. Invisible line, invisible hook. Get the monster inside this book!"

The monster hunter braced for the inevitable force of magic. He shut his eyes against the anticipated roar of the beast. When none came, he opened his eyes, searching for the creature. There was nothing. Confounded, Marius checked the pages of his book. There was nothing there but the word *Rougarou*.

It wasn't until he heard the rumble behind him that he knew where the monster had gone. The sound reminded Marius of rolling thunder building strength inside a thunderhead. The growl expanded in the creature's chest until it lashed out with an explosion of motion.

The rougarou roared so loud it made Marius's ears pop. A red light exploded from the creature's throat, temporarily blinding the monster hunter. It scooped a mass of dirt and pebbles in its massive paw and threw it at Marius. Not only did it knock him to the ground, but it also broke the salt circle protecting him. Grit and rocks rained on his body.

He heard the beating sound of the rougarou running at him before he got his sight back. Marius grabbed his book and rolled to the right. He opened his eyes just in time to see the monster claw open the patch of earth where he had just been. It turned its white face to him. Those hard, black stones for eyes stared into Marius's soul, and he knew that tonight he was going to die.

Marius got up, grabbed a handful of brick dust, and tossed it into the rougarou's eyes. It barely noticed. A few quick blinks and that was it. Marius turned from the shore and made to run into the clearing, but he did not get far. The rougarou knocked him down from behind and clamped down on his ankle with one clawed hand.

He screamed when the beast squeezed his leg. It was pure, searing agony. Marius struggled against it, beating on the monster's back, but it did nothing. Might as well try to punch a brick wall. When the rougarou flung Marius, he heard something in his ankle crack. He did not know which bones were giving way, but one of them snapped.

Marius landed near the water broken and battered. He felt utterly helpless. The rougarou loomed over him. Marius braced himself for the killing blow, but instead, the beast grabbed his arm and tossed him aside again. Luckily, nothing broke as his body slammed against the hard-packed earth once again. The wind was knocked out of him, and he gasped for breath.

When the rougarou went to do it again, Marius realized something important. The rougarou was playing with him the way a cat played with a mouse. This was fun for it. Something about that made Marius furious. He was not some plaything. His life was worth more than that, and he would hurt this monster if it was the last thing he did.

When Marius felt the rougarou reach for his broken ankle again, he brought his fillet knife from his pocket and stabbed it as hard as he could. He managed to lodge the blade just behind the beast's wolfish ear. It shrieked and threw Marius away. As soon as he hit the ground, Marius sat up, armed with nothing but his flask of salt.

"Come on, you dog-ugly sack of puke. Come get me!" Marius screamed.

The rougarou roared at him. Marius's knife still stuck out behind its ear. It did not try to pull it out. All of the beast's attention was on killing the monster hunter. It charged Marius. He threw salt at the monster, but it barely slowed it down. Marius threw his hands over his head and awaited the rougarou's horrible teeth.

Nothing happened.

Marius heard a sharp whine and then a series of short, snapping growls. He opened his eyes to see the rougarou thrashing around on the beach with something attached to its shoulder. The great thing roared and whimpered and clawed desperately at something Marius could not make out.

As soon as the rougarou moved into the moonlight, Marius saw Rhiannon. She was latched on to the beast's shoulder with all of her many teeth. Her claws dug and tore into its flesh. When the rougarou pulled one of her claws free, she pushed her barb directly in its back. Again and again, she attacked like the fierce monster she was.

Marius realized how near he was to the deeper water. Rhiannon must have followed him. She made her way here to help. A rising hope swelled in his chest. It warmed him from the inside out, giving him enough strength to keep going.

He was not alone.

The monster hunter rolled over onto his knees and managed to balance on one foot. If he could get to his book, he could end this. He spotted the remains of his salt circle about ten yards away. The book lay lifeless in the middle of it. His broken ankle screamed at him as he hobbled away.

Before Marius reached the book, the rougarou got the better of Rhiannon. With a terrible raking motion, the beast clawed her, peeling her off its back. It grabbed the mermaid by the tail and flung her toward Marius. She hit the ground in front of him with a wet gasp. Dark red claw marks ran up her right arm and across her chest.

She did not move. Her mouth was normal again, her barbs were retracted, and she looked so small in the dirt. Marius could not tell if she was breathing at all.

"Rhia!" Marius screamed.

With a guttural roar, the rougarou charged toward them both. Marius crawled as fast as he could to get in between the beast and Rhiannon.

"Marius, the amulet!"

It was all he had left. One last-ditch effort. He had no idea what it would do, or if it would do anything at all, but his mother said it would help. If nothing happened, at least he would die defending a friend. Neither of them would be alone.

Marius dug inside his shirt and pulled out the raven pendant. The rougarou's fangs were so close he could smell the hot stench of its breath on his skin. He snapped the chain and held it toward the monster.

Everything went white.

CHAPTER TWENTY-SEVEN

For some reason, being temporarily blinded made your ears ring. That should not be. It didn't make sense, yet Marius found himself with his hands over his ears as the world came back into focus. The whining tone in his head dissipated slowly as he took in the scene.

First of all, he was not dead. That was good because he had expected to be dead. The second thing he noticed was that the rougarou was not dead either. It lay in a heap nearby, panting loudly and whimpering. The third thing was that Rhiannon might be dead because she was not moving.

"No. No, no, no," Marius said, crawling toward the mermaid. "Rhia, talk to me! No, you can't be dead. Why did you come looking for me? You could have just let me die."

Marius looked her over and gently touched her uninjured shoulder. The scratches along her arm and collarbone were deep. Reddish-black blood oozed from within. He put his head to her chest and felt the tiniest thrum of a heartbeat. It was weak and slow, but it was there.

There were remnants of her rosary scattered on the beach around her. The cord was broken. Little skull beads littered the ground. Something dropped in his stomach. It was her protection, and now it was gone.

The rougarou moaned and snarled in a mass about ten yards away. It sounded like a fraction of the monster it had been moments before. Even though the beast was laid low, Marius was not sure for how long. Its growls were labored, and its breathing came out in short bursts. He wanted to stay with Rhiannon. Someone had to help her, but the rougarou was still a danger. He had to slay the beast now, or they might both die.

Marius clutched the raven skull amulet in his hand. The silver glinted in the evening's light. The moonstone inlaid on the top glowed white hot from whatever spell Marius had unleashed. His mother was right. It was powerful enough to protect him, but for how long? He scanned the area, but could not locate his monster book.

There was a long, forked stick nearby. Marius used it as a crutch to hobble over to the rougarou. He approached carefully. The monster was a pile of whimpering fur and scales. When he got close, he saw the rigid alligator spines along the back of the creature. Scaled, tough skin woven in with black fur.

He smelled the mildew odor of stagnant water. The tang of blood and electricity was in the air. Marius had not noticed it before, but the rougarou had bayou moss and weeds woven in with the top of its fur. Deep puncture wounds lined its shoulders and back. Whole chunks of flesh were missing thanks to Rhiannon's mouth full of teeth.

Without the book, there was no way to trap it. He would have to incapacitate it some other way. Thread. His mother said the beast was held together by thread.

Carefully, Marius limped his way around the beast. Its white face shone in the moonlight as its head moved back and forth, snapping here and there at the different sounds. The dark stone eyes were now a pinkish red. The rougarou moved them wildly, as if trying to find something that was invisible.

"You're blind now," Marius whispered.

The rougarou's face whipped toward him, snapping at the empty air between them. It tried to move its arms, but Rhiannon had done quite a number on the beast. Marius saw a splatter of blood on its white face just above its ear. In silhouette, it looked like the rougarou had three ears. The third ear was, in fact, Marius's knife still sticking out of the monster's head.

Marius's plan was completely foolish, but it was all he had. He limped around to the rear end of the creature. With one long jump, he managed to catapult his body onto its back. The rougarou was crippled, but it still roared and thrashed. Marius dug his hand into the mossy fur and clenched his legs as best he could so he would not get thrown.

When the beast fell on its stomach again, Marius clawed

his way toward its neck. He dug his good foot into the monster's injured shoulder, hobbling it with pain. It whimpered and snapped at him, but Marius felt in control. He grabbed his blade and yanked it out. A loud roar echoed in the silence of the bayou.

With the knife came a section of fur and flesh. A tiny glimmer caught the moonlight beneath the blood and gore. A thread. It was a golden thread stitched just below its ear. Marius might have jumped for joy if he were able. This was the thread his mother had told him about. This could be its undoing.

Marius jabbed his knife into the mass of stitching. With one quick yank, the string broke. The beast screamed as he grabbed one of the ends and pulled it back hard. It was like unraveling a horrible sweater. He pulled and pulled on the bloody twine. Within seconds, the beast's ear tumbled off.

The injured monster hunter rolled off the rougarou with the thread still in hand. He backed away, pulling as hard as he could. It roared one last time before its snout broke away and fell to the ground. Next was the head and the shoulders down to the torso and the haunches. Marius kept pulling and pulling until the creature was nothing more than a mass of heaving parts.

There was a faint glow coming from beneath the rougarou's right arm. Marius limped toward it, easily dodging the writhing muscles and useless claws. When he spotted the source of the light, relief washed over him. It was his monster book.

Marius panted heavily as he pried the volume from underneath the creature. His lungs filled with the hot stench of wet dog and sweat when the book came free. Deep, endless relief flooded his body.

Marius crawled away and sat in the soggy grass. He opened to the correct page and pointed it at the rougarou. It was such a useless lump of flesh now, but he would still collect it. Marius licked his dry lips and began.

"Grab the arm, grab the crook. Stomp the ground until it's shook. Invisible line, invisible hook. Get the monster inside this book!"

Unlike all of his other monsters, the rougarou did not wail as the power sucked it inside the pages. There was no fighting, no scratching at the earth in vain. The lifeless lump of parts vanished inside the pages with no more resistance than dirt into a vacuum cleaner.

Marius sucked in a deep sigh of relief, but he did not have long to linger. There was still Rhiannon. She had not moved during all of this. When he crawled back over to her, the light pulse she had was gone.

"No. No, I took too long. Rhia, come on! Can you hear me?"

The mermaid did not move. Not a flutter of eyelids or a rise of her chest. Marius felt a chilling panic throughout his bones. It was his fault. She would not have been here if it were not for him. He had to bring her back.

Feeling the weight of the knife in his hand reminded him of something important. Mermaid hair was the best bandage in the world. Marius sliced a handful of her longest tendrils at the bottom and lined them over her wounds. One at a time, making sure they were properly affixed.

Her blood no longer wept from the gash in her shoulder, but she still was not breathing. Marius dragged her body the few feet into the shallow water. Most people did not know where mermaid gills were, but Marius knew. He felt behind her ears and pulled gently until the delicate lines opened. He splashed handful after handful of water inside.

Still, she did not respond.

"What is it? What can I do? There has to be something!"

Marius twisted this way and that, searching the swamp for a clue, any clue. He came up empty, and Rhiannon's body was growing cold.

"Mom! What do I do?"

Marius waited, but his mother's voice did not appear. No one was here to help him. They were the only people for miles, and even then, who would help a mermaid? No one knew her but him. No one loved her but him.

The calling spell, it was his only chance.

He knew the spell by heart. Everyone knew it in their world. Most normal children learned how to dial the correct emergency number. Perhaps they memorized family allergies and emergency contacts. Children like Marius were taught spells that healed cuts, soothed burns, and called recently departed souls back to their bodies.

There was no exact time limit for the calling spell that brought a loved one's soul back to their body. So many factors were at play. A good rule of thumb was twenty minutes. If you could not get to them in twenty minutes, there was little chance of bringing them back.

Unlike his resurrection spell, the calling spell was easy. It was the same one Madame Millet performed on her husband when she found him dead of a heart attack. It was the same one Marius tried to perform on his mother after the car accident. Both times were fruitless because the person's soul had already passed. But maybe, just maybe, it would work now.

"Dead and dying, no flesh or glove. Drifting over the world above. Wax is melting, wounded dove. Return thine body, my friend and love!"

Nothing happened.

There had to be a way, he thought. There just had to be.

He spotted the raven skull necklace nearby next to where he had dropped his monster book. It glinted brightly, as if summoning him. The moonstone radiated white light. A hopeful idea blossomed inside his mind. It was a long shot, but maybe it would work.

Marius grabbed the talisman and scrambled back over

to Rhiannon. His ankle was killing him, but he could not worry about that now. He pulled more of her body into the water to keep her tail from drying out. It was already losing some of its luminescence. With trembling fingers, Marius tied the raven skull around Rhiannon's neck.

A terrible thought crossed his mind, and he froze in place. What if this was the opposite of helping? The raven skull had incapacitated the rougarou. Rhiannon was a monster. She was his friend but technically a monster. He didn't know how this worked.

Rhiannon's color faded further. Time was running out. He had to act.

Marius readjusted the talisman on her chest. He splashed some more murky water on her lifeless body. No, he thought. He could not start thinking of her as a body. That was a sure-fire way to fail. She was Rhiannon. Not a body. Not yet.

Marius faced the mermaid with renewed intention. He clapped the air above Rhiannon's chest. Even though the night sky was clear, a roar of thunder bellowed when his hands met. He rubbed them together, feeling a charge. Marius gazed down at his friend and placed his hands on her shoulders.

"Dead and dying, no flesh or glove. Drifting over the world above. Wax is melting, wounded dove. Return thine body, my friend and love!"

Again, the world flashed white, and Marius saw nothing.

CHAPTER TWENTY-EIGHT

Marius fell onto his back, holding his eyes. The sand and pebbles ground against his scalp. There was that ringing again, but it did not last as long. He removed his hands from his face and tried to focus.

At first, the world stayed white. He wondered if this time the amulet had blinded him the way it had the rougarou. Luckily, he did not wonder for more than a few seconds.

The world darkened and righted itself for him. He saw the trees above and the stars in the night sky. Water soaked him up to his waist. There were still spots in his eyes, but they were fading.

Marius flipped over in a panic to check Rhiannon. He grabbed her wrists and patted her face. He pressed his ear to her chest again but came up with no pulse at all. The bandages still adhered to her wounds, but that was it. Her face did not move. He looked at her hard, willing her chest to rise. It refused.

Marius dug his fingers into the dirt and screamed into the buzzing Louisiana air. *Why not*, he thought. Who cared if he howled? There were no monsters left. All of them were gone, even the mermaid. He collapsed back onto the ground and covered his face with filthy hands. He wanted to cry. He might have cried if he had anything left.

When he felt the tiny coolness on his forehead, he nearly jumped out of his skin. It was the feathery touch of a mermaid's kiss. He might be the only human to know what that felt like and still be breathing. Marius pulled his hands away from his face to see Rhiannon smiling down at him.

"Hi," she said with a raspy voice. "I think I might have been dead just now."

Marius didn't say a word. He sat up with his mouth hanging open. Then, in one fast motion, he threw his arms around her and squeezed tightly.

"I thought I lost you," he said.

"Ouch, ouch! Careful!" she shouted.

Marius pulled away with his own shock of pain and apologized. In all his excitement, he had crushed her wounded shoulder. They were quite the pair, injured and pitiful. The good news was they were alive. Marius hugged her again, much more carefully.

"You were gone. It was all my fault, and you were gone," he whispered into her hair. "Why did you come for me?"

"We are friends. That's what friends do, don't they?" she asked.

"I don't know many friends who would take on a rougarou for someone else," Marius pointed out.

"I don't know many humans who would save a mermaid," Rhiannon said.

They sat in the shallow water together, taking in what had happened. The gentle movement of the bayou felt good against his body, reminding him that the world still turned. They survived.

Something, maybe a fish, moved past Marius's broken ankle, causing him to flinch. He winced in pain. As if connected, Rhiannon too flinched, holding her shoulder.

"Did you feel that?" he asked.

"Yes. Can you feel this?" she asked, pressing on her shoulder.

"Ouch! Yes. Don't do that," he said.

Marius and Rhiannon stared blankly at each other's injuries. The air between them swirled in a surreal way. A touch of magic that was not there before. For some reason, his ankle and her shoulder felt the same pain.

"Well, that's a new one," Rhiannon said, turning her gaze to her wound.

"Yes," Marius agreed. "A new one indeed."

Getting out of the swamp took most of the night. Marius had to hold Rhiannon around the waist and use a large stick to move through the water. When he got tired, the mermaid took over, dragging him along in the deeper parts when they presented themselves. Everything was made worse by the fact that anytime his ankle hurt, her shoulder would give way, and vice versa. Whatever the reason, their wounds at the hand of the rougarou were magically linked.

The boat was a welcomed sight but also hard to maneuver injured. Throwing his broken ankle over the edge hurt worse than he anticipated, making him howl with pain. The mermaid gritted her teeth underwater until he got settled.

Once Marius positioned himself inside, he cast the line for Rhiannon to hang on to. Even though he was exhausted, he was able to row without much pain, so he had her just hang on with her good arm while he dragged her through the water.

They reached the Greystone Cemetery just as the sun peeked its head over the horizon. When Marius spotted the dock to his little graveyard, he felt like the happiest person in the world. They'd done it. They'd survived. Now he could get his mother back.

CHAPTER
TWENTY-NINE

When he limped up to Madame Millet's front door, he was soaked through with bayou water and caked all over with grave dust. He reeked of filth and blood. Even her ornery cats gave him a wide berth.

After the battle, his first inclination was to go home and sleep. The problem was that he did not have much time left before the spell was forfeit. Plus, his ankle was definitely broken. His next idea was to go to the Habada-Chérie to cash the rougarou in with Papa Harold. That was too far to go alone. He would never make it.

Madame Millet's house was two houses down from the graveyard. A much easier walk after grave hopping. So, Madame Millet's house it was.

Marius rang the doorbell. He prayed silently that Madame Millet would open the door. It would be fine if one of the twins answered. Anybody except . . .

"What hellcat coughed you up, Mary?"

Anybody except Mildred.

There were only so many words left in his brain after his ordeal, and Marius decided he did not want to waste any of them on Mildred Millet. He said nothing as she paused to fully take him in. Mildred's mouth fell open when she saw the blood on his clothes, and she stepped back to avoid the bayou water puddling around his feet.

"You . . . actually did it?"

A gust of sandalwood-scented air blew past them as Madame Millet filled the doorway behind her daughter. She took one look at Marius and swept him inside, pushing Mildred out of the way.

"Oh my God, what happened? What did this to you?" Madame Millet cried in a panic.

He didn't answer at first. All the movement left him in a considerable amount of pain. The great woman threw his arm over her shoulder and helped him maneuver through the hall and into her parlor. The same one where Marius had stolen virgin water before. He felt guilty all over again.

She forced Marius into one of her nice chairs. He knew he was soaking her fancy cushions with bayou water and blood, but somehow, he didn't much care. Madame Millet didn't seem to mind, so why should he.

"Answer," she demanded as she inspected his wounds.

"I was hunting a rougarou," Marius said weakly.

Might as well come clean, he thought.

He spotted Mildred lurking near the door. Her face was

filled with a mixture of fear and awe. She did not shoot any of her usual glares his way. If anything, she looked terrified.

"A rougarou! You foolish child. What gave you that idea? It could have killed you."

"It almost did," Marius said. "But I got it first."

Marius produced the monster book from his pocket and dropped it on the table with a hard *thunk*. The volume had seen better days. It was worn and a tad waterlogged. The pages were crumpled around the edges, but they still hummed and pulsated with the light of the rougarou inside. Luckily, monster books healed themselves with time, much like a human, but this one in particular had just gone through the ringer. It would take some time to recover.

"You . . . caught a rougarou?" Madame Millet said, staring at the book.

Madame Millet grabbed the phone mounted on the wall, and dialed. She never took her eyes off Marius as she did.

"Yes, hello. My name is Madge Millet, and I need an ambulance," she said.

There was no need to give an address. Marius was quite sure Madame Millet never gave out her address to anyone. There was not a person in Algiers Point that did not know her house. Fear her or love her, you knew where she lived.

"I have a boy here who was . . . attacked by a wild dog. Yes, in the bayou somewhere. I don't know where. Just get here immediately!"

Madame Millet hung up the phone and gave Mildred

a worried look. They stared at Marius like he was going to sprout three heads and twist his neck around.

"I'm not going anywhere until I collect my bounty," he said flatly.

Mildred and her mother stared at the glowing pages of the book. As though recognizing it was being watched, the book vibrated harder, shaking the baubles on the table. A ghostly echo of a rougarou howl filled the small room. The women jumped.

"You actually caught it?" Mildred asked.

"Yep."

"You mean to tell me that you collected a rougarou in that book?" Madame Millet asked slowly and with great caution.

"Yes. Now I want to get paid. I'm not going to any hospital until that happens."

"How am I supposed to pay you?" Madame Millet asked.

"I was in your storeroom," he said with more than a little shame dancing across his face. "I saw the scales in the back."

Had Marius not been in a world of pain, he might have laughed at Madame Millet's face. It was rare to see the great lady so unnerved, but now, she was positively stunned. She did not try to deny it though.

Without another word, Madame Millet got up and disappeared into her storeroom. When she returned, there was an old set of scales in her hands. She sat down across from him and presented her scales on the table. It was her turn to look ashamed.

"Maman?" Mildred asked with a world of questions in her tone.

"It was a long time ago, child," was her only answer.

"Maman, I can hear the sirens," Mildred said.

They all heard it. The ambulance was maybe a few blocks away, whining its annoying song into the wee hours of the morning. Madame Millet quickened her pace, gesturing for Marius to place the book on the plate. He did so, and she hurriedly moved the weights around.

She added weight after weight after weight on the scales, but it did not balance with the worth of the monster. Madame Millet went through every weight she had, and it still was not enough. She finally gave up, throwing her heavily beaded necklace on the scale as well.

Apparently, that was finally enough. The copper penny transformed into a Mystic coin. The value on the top read four hundred.

Marius breathed out a long sigh of relief. It was more than he needed, he thought. He finally had the last part of the spell. He took the coin and his book, replacing them both in his coat. With them secured, he slumped down into the chair, feeling every ounce of how tired he was.

"Child, how on earth did you do this?" Madame Millet asked.

She never got an answer. The whining of the ambulance siren took over all the sound in the room. It was now right outside, and two paramedics rushed into the house.

Mildred leaped out of the way as they surrounded Marius, checking his body and shining lights in his eyes.

"It's his right ankle," Mildred said from the doorway.

"What happened to him? What is he covered in?" the paramedic asked.

"We don't know," Madame Millet said. "He came home like this. Said something about a big dog. I'm his . . . auntie, so I can ride along with you."

"Son, can you hear us?" asked the other paramedic.

"It's my ankle that's broken. Not my ears," Marius said.

He heard Mildred snort, and Madame Millet shooed her away, whispering something about watching the twins and taking care of the house. One paramedic touched Marius's ankle, and he jolted with the pain. The other was checking the rest of his body. He must have been a mess. They kept giving each other strange looks.

It took some effort, but they managed to get Marius on a stretcher and load him into the ambulance. He was not fond of the oxygen mask or the IV. What he did like was the pain medication. It slithered into his veins, cold and soothing, without him even knowing it.

For the first time since the fight, Marius felt no pain at all. It was so relieving, he drifted effortlessly to sleep. He just hoped somewhere Rhiannon was getting the benefit of it too.

CHAPTER THIRTY

A day and a half passed before Marius found himself standing in front of his cemetery's sign again. Granted, it was not how he would have liked to come home. He balanced himself on a borrowed set of crutches. His right ankle had a blue cast on it, and he was wearing borrowed scrubs from the hospital. Marius's clothes had been deemed unsalvageable, except for his oversized coat, which seemed to fare well, all things considered. He refused to part with it.

The wild dog story had finally placated the doctors and authorities. Madame "Auntie" Millet got him released as soon as she was able. The great woman collected and paid his bill, all evidence he was ever there. Charts, notes, receipts. She had the clout to make it all disappear.

Of course, Madame Millet tried to tempt him into staying with her for a few days to recover, but Marius declined politely. The thought of sharing a roof with Mildred for any amount of time was utterly distasteful.

Marius was not great on the crutches, but it beat a

random stick in a swamp, so who was he to complain? He pushed himself along as the sun hung low in the sky. It would be sundown soon, and the ghosts would have a million questions for him. He needed to act soon.

Hugo stepped out from behind a tomb with a fearful look on his face. Ghosts did not wear fear well. Why should they be afraid of anything? They were already dead. Hugo did not say a word as Marius approached. He just pointed a trembling finger toward the dock. Marius did not need further explanation.

Limping with crutches on a dirt path was a lot easier than using them on an uneven wooden dock, but Marius managed. When he got close to the edge, he put them aside and scooted close to the water. The boat was tethered to the side, allowing for an empty space in front of him.

She emerged slowly but steadily. The water beneath the dock was shallower, but there was enough room for her to maneuver through the tall grass. Rhiannon reached her good hand up, grabbed the dock's edge, and pulled herself to the surface. Those aquamarine eyes of hers danced as she took him in.

"They put a weird thing on your foot," she said while thumping his cast with one of her claws.

"It's to keep it still, so it heals."

"Humans are so strange," she said.

"How's the shoulder?" he asked. "Do you think they are still linked?"

Rhiannon did not answer with words. She poked her bandaged shoulder instead. Marius and Rhiannon both winced in pain at the same time. Their injuries were still magically connected, even after some healing.

"I guess so," Marius said.

There were a myriad of words that needed to be said. Hours and hours of conversation. So much had happened. So many things had changed. They needed to talk about it. Discussing it would be the healthy way to process such a traumatic event.

Neither said a word.

Marius and Rhiannon sat in silence together. Not uncomfortably. Not angrily. They just decided to breathe in a few beautiful minutes together without words. In the end, they did not need to talk about the night with the rougarou. At least, not just yet. It was enough to share the air together, knowing they had both made it out alive.

As the day turned into dusk, Marius glanced over toward his cemetery. There was still one more thing to do. He was afraid and excited but could not bring himself to move.

"She's waiting for you," Rhiannon said, breaking the silence.

"Yes. I don't know what I'm waiting for," he said.

"You're waiting for this," she said.

He turned back to the mermaid as she pulled his raven skull talisman from around her neck. The moonstone had stopped shining the night of the battle. It appeared now as it always did. Beautiful and unassuming. Rhiannon placed it in his hands.

"But what if you need it to heal?" he asked. "I'm not sure how this thing works, and your rosary broke during the fight."

"I'm fine. Besides, you might need it to call her back. And you can get me a new necklace. I like the skulls in the last one better anyway," she said.

"I don't know how to thank you," Marius said with a smile.

"Then don't right now," she said simply. "Thank me when you do know how. Otherwise, it's just wasted time trying."

Marius smiled wider and nodded. He stuffed the raven skull inside his coat pocket. It took some effort, but he managed to stand up and collect his crutches underneath his arms. He gave Rhiannon a quick wave, and she waved back just before she dove under the water. The sudden surge of water on her shoulder caused his ankle to ache.

He hobbled awkwardly to his family mausoleum. The crutches made it difficult to open the ancient doors, but he found a way. Marius took a long pull from a bottle of water and retrieved his supplies. Mystic coins, raven skull, candles, stolen spell, brick dust, salt, and a crowbar.

Marius pried the headstone away from the wall of the tomb. Kelly Stone's name fell to the earth with her grave marker. Then he pulled out the bricks behind it. He peered inside the empty grave. His mother had been entombed almost two years ago, so her body was nothing more than ash and tiny bone fragments. Nothing recognizable.

Staring into a familiar grave felt like looking into a skull's eye socket. A dark, cavernous void that used to hold something important. Now the life was gone. The necessary things laid to dust. Reversing the tide was going to be a difficult task.

Marius checked the stolen spell pages and followed the prep work exactly. This was more than simply calling the soul back to a recently dead person. This spell brought someone back from an afterlife. There was no body left to return to. Kelly Stone's body was nothing but ash. He had to pull her out of Hell, body and soul.

He marked the wall around the opening with three *X*s on each side in brick dust. He drew a half circle on the ground in front of the grave in salt. He lit white candles and placed them on every windowsill and door. Next, he stacked the Mystic coins needed. The sum had to be exactly six hundred and sixty-six coins. It was a high number, but that was Hell's price.

The final part was not written in the spell, but it was something necessary. Rhiannon had reaffirmed that idea. Marius took the raven skull necklace and placed it just inside his mother's grave. What better talisman to call her back to the living? A bit of her ashes stuck to his fingers, and he didn't have the heart to wipe it away.

Marius stood back from his work and took a deep

breath. The words had to be recited perfectly. There was no room to stutter or hesitate. He read the spell several times in his head before he said it aloud.

"Angel's wing, demon's bait. Take the lives of ones who wait. Crooked tails, lies so straight. Allow this soul through Hell's cursed gate."

A heavy wind blew the doors open, snuffing out the candles inside the mausoleum. Only moments before, there had been nary a breeze, and now a gale forced its way inside. It battered the stained glass windows, but they held strong. Marius jumped, but he began again.

"Angel's wing, demon's bait. Take the lives of ones who wait. Crooked tails, lies so straight. Allow this soul through Hell's cursed gate."

Outside of the mausoleum was the sound of an explosion, but one that seemed to come from all sides at once. The force of the blast blew the windows inward. Marius ducked and protected his head with his hands. It felt like someone had lit fireworks on either side of the building. A rain of glass shards sprayed toward Marius, dusting him in fine glass and dirt.

He stood back up, undaunted. Calm did not return, but he had to continue. There was one more incantation he had to do, but the wind screamed around the room, biting at his skin. The salt half circle broke from the explosion, but he could not fix it. There was not time. He had to move forward, or all would be lost.

"Angel's wing, demon's bait. Take the lives of ones who wait. Crooked tails, lies so straight. Allow this soul through Hell's cursed gate!"

He expected one last explosion. One final attempt to kill him or stop the spell from happening. Perhaps the crossroad demon who took her would appear to fight Marius over the state of his mother's soul. He was ready. He would fight anything no matter how injured.

Nothing happened.

The shrieking wind and terrible explosion snuffed away as quickly as they appeared. The destruction remained, but the cause vanished. All the evil energy had been sucked from the room. Candles littered the floor among the glass shards. Brick dust and salt covered his shoe and cast. Marius stared into his mother's grave and there was nothing. No red light from within. No mother returning to him. Nothing. Just darkness.

The spell did not work.

He sat on the floor amid the terrible silence. Somehow, the world seemed emptier than before. The lack of her breath, of her voice, of the cadence of her breathing hit harder. Before all of this, she had not been fully gone, not to him. When there was a chance the spell could work, she was still somewhat alive. Now? Now it was all over. His mother was truly and completely gone. He would never get her back from Hell.

Marius buried his face in his hands and wept. They were not the loud, racking sobs of a child. No, he was not that anymore. He had not been for some time, even when he wanted to be. His tears ran steadily and quietly down his cheeks. It was the way of orphans who do not get to be children anymore.

"I'm so sorry, Mom. I failed you," he said.

CHAPTER THIRTY-ONE

When he limped out of the mausoleum, the world was as he had left it. Nothing changed. That fact felt wrong somehow. All the effort and pain should have leaked into the fiber of the universe around him; or so he thought. It should have meant something somewhere.

"It doesn't revolve around you, son. It doesn't revolve around me. It doesn't revolve around anybody."

He breathed in the dank air and the tangy scent of salt on his clothes. The last strips of daylight were fading away. Lightning bugs joined the dragonflies as they buzzed across the water's surface.

Marius spotted Hugo and Rhiannon on the dock. They whispered to each other. When they spotted him, they both perked up. Each wore their own version of a hopeful face. Hugo's had all the unbridled optimism of a child. Rhiannon's eyes were so wide they almost looked cartoonish.

It made his stomach turn all the more when they saw his expression. He witnessed the hope drain from them like it had for him. All the work and pain and danger was for nothing. They had failed. No, he had failed them.

No one said a word as he made his way slowly to the dock. It was not until he plopped on the edge that Hugo dared to speak.

"What happened?"

Marius could not bring himself to answer. It was all just too much.

"It did not work," Rhiannon said, answering on his behalf. "Did it?"

He shook his head and slumped against one of the dock supports. Marius could not bring himself to look at the mermaid. She'd nearly died helping him, and for what? Nothing.

"Marius?" Hugo asked tentatively.

"I . . . I can't talk about it right now," Marius said.

His voice sounded weak and pitiful. *Might as well*, he thought. It was how he felt.

"But, Marius . . . ," Hugo said again.

"Not now, Hugo. I . . ."

"Marius!" Rhiannon said. It came out so suddenly and sharp, both he and Hugo jolted in place. "Turn around now!"

The monster hunter whipped his head around, and saw a stranger standing in his cemetery. He was odd-looking. Pale, but not like it was his normal skin tone. More like he was ill, or someone had drained the blood from his body.

The man's eyes were bloodshot and bulging. He slumped over like something in his stomach pained him.

Marius used the post to pull himself to his feet. Rhiannon grabbed the dock with both hands. She clenched her teeth and tensed all over. He felt the pain in his ankle from her efforts.

"Hugo, get out of here," Marius said when the man started twitching.

The lutin vanished into thin air. Marius hoped he would stay that way. Not many things could hurt ghosts, but he was not about to test that now. There was no telling what kind of threat they were facing.

"You are the boy?" the stranger asked through gritted teeth. He seemed genuinely in pain, like he was holding something in, and the effort was hurting him. "The mo . . . mon . . . monster-hunter boy?"

"That's me," Marius said slowly. "Who are you?"

The strange man did not answer. Instead, he screamed and began to change into something else. His body convulsed as he grew taller and thinner. His arms elongated and his nails sharpened into talons. Skin peeled away from his face as the skull of a deer replaced his own head. Antlers sprouted on top as his eyes sank into the skull, only to be replaced by glowing red orbs. Bloody clothes littered the ground around him.

When the deed was done, the monster stood fifteen feet tall. All clothing had ripped and fallen around his hooves.

His emaciated body slumped much like it had before, but now, they could see each exposed rib and flesh falling from his torso. He was all bones, claws, and patches of fur. No sign of the man remained.

"What is that?" Rhiannon hissed.

"A wendigo," Marius whispered to her. "Mom told me about them. He's not supposed to be here. They don't live this far south."

The monster stood up straight for the first time and growled at them. Marius reached into his pocket and grabbed his monster book. His body ached as his did so. He could feel his still-healing bones creak.

The wendigo clawed at the ground and stamped his hoof like a bull about to charge a matador. Marius readied himself for another fight, but before the monster could spring into action, it crumpled to the ground, moaning from some unseen injury.

Much to everyone's surprise, Rex appeared from behind the beast. The demon wore that sly grin he always had. The one that made Marius's skin crawl. The monster hunter slipped the book back into his pocket but did not remove his hand.

"There will be none of that, Hector," Rex said as he grabbed the wendigo's antler and pulled him to the ground. "We are here to pay a debt."

The wendigo groaned pitifully. Rex released him, and the creature righted himself on all fours. Those glowing eyes shot from Rex to the monster hunter and then back again.

"What are you talking about? What debt?" Marius asked.

His back molars hurt from grinding. He eased his muscles, popping his jaw as he did so. Marius focused all his tension on gripping his book. At that point he could not tell where to point it. Who was the real danger?

He decided to keep the book hidden until he knew. Better not to show his hand. What if Rex decided to try and take it?

"You paid Hell quite the price, baby hunter. We pay our debts."

"But the spell didn't work."

"Ah yes, the spell," Rex said with a little chuckle. "You did everything correctly, except one major issue."

"And what's that?" he asked.

"You didn't have a body for her. She's all ashes, child," Rex said as his smile lit up his fierce eyes. He held out his hand to reveal a small pile of ashes. "Where did you think her soul was going to go when you called her back?"

"I . . . didn't . . ."

Something in his gut told him the ashes in Rex's hand belonged to his mother. He gazed down at his own fingers. They still had remnants of the ashes he had touched earlier.

Marius was speechless and angry. He didn't know she needed a body to come back to, but as he thought about it, the demon made sense. Marius absolutely hated that fact, and he scowled at the smug creature. Rex's glee in seeing his embarrassment made it so much worse. Marius decided to change direction.

"Since when does Hell pays its debts, anyway? Your kind swindled my mother in the first place. You didn't live up to your deal then."

"Oh, is that what you were told?"

"That's what I know," Marius spat back.

"Well, kid, you might want to get some facts straight. It's a lucky day for you, of course. You can ask your dear mother yourself. Get the real story from the horse's mouth and all that."

Before Marius could say another word, Rex grabbed the wendigo by the antler again and pushed him forward. He stumbled and whimpered. Marius almost felt sorry for the monster.

"Do it," Rex said.

"I don't want to. I've paid my bill," the wendigo said back.

The beast's voice sounded like gravel rolling around in a tin can. It echoed from within the hollow parts of the stag skull.

"You have a long way to go before you're in the black, Hector. Do it now, or I will do it for you," Rex said. His smile never left his face.

"What is happening?" Marius asked.

He spared a look at Rhiannon to see if she had any ideas. To his relief, she had moved on the other side of the dock's support post. A place where she could hide but also see what was happening. Rex had not noticed her, and that was best.

She had one pale hand wrapped around the post with her sharp nails dug into the wood. Her eyes trained on the scene in front of them. Marius knew that if he needed the mermaid, she would spring into action without hesitation.

The wendigo whimpered again and stamped the ground. He reached into his chest and yanked hard. A sickening *crack* cut through the air. When the monster pulled his hand out, he held one of his own ribs.

A strong breeze blew through the graveyard, wafting the stench from the wendigo's body. It reminded Marius of the boo hag. All rot and ruin beneath strips of flesh. The difference being the wendigo was covered in patches of fur. The smell brought images of a mangy corpse lying out in the hot sun. He held his hand over his nose.

The monster began digging in the soggy ground. With those large talons, it did not take long to make a sizable hole. He dropped the rib inside. When the wendigo was done, he limped backward, cowering behind the demon. Thick, brownish blood oozed from his chest.

Rex glided toward the hole and added his handful of ashes on top of the rib. A deep shudder racked Marius's body, vibrating his injured ankle inside its cast. The demon filled in the hole with the remaining dirt, leaving a small mound.

"Do you know how a wendigo is made?" Rex asked without any explanation for what had just happened.

"It's a corrupted person that's been cursed. A cannibal," Marius said. He was not happy about this school-like scenario, but he played along to get to the point faster.

"After the change, they are never satisfied, you know. Always hungry. They feast on humans, but it's never enough. Old Hector here has eaten dozens, maybe hundreds, of people in his lifetime."

"What has that got to do with my mother?"

"One bone from a wendigo has enough raw material to grow a whole human," Rex said, gesturing to the small mound of earth that held the rib and ashes. "Hell pays its debts. We will make a body for your mother."

CHAPTER THIRTY-TWO

Rex snapped a finger, and the ground began to rumble. It shook the trees and made the boards on the dock chatter together like the teeth in Marius's head. He held on to the support post for dear life, trying to lessen the pain in his ankle. He had the urge to move onto dry land, but Rhiannon was at the dock. Together, they were safer.

Eventually, the rumble faded into a tremor, which faded into stillness once again. The only evidence of their little earthquake was the new litter of leaves on the ground. The wendigo and demon appeared unaffected.

There was a long pause where no one said a word. In fact, nothing said a word. There were no crickets. No splashing fish. No frogs singing. No breeze. The water from the bayou rested, stiller than he had ever seen.

The silence felt worse than the earthquake. It was like something had sucked all of the air from the area, and no one could breathe. Marius was about to say something, anything to get the world talking again. Turns out, he did not have to do a thing. Someone else gave the world back its voice.

The mound moved. The earth quivered and pushed. It expanded and pressed upward, like a boil about to burst. After a few seconds, one slender hand shot out, spewing bits of soil and leaves in all directions. A second hand followed shortly after. They clawed and pushed until a head appeared. The rest of the body followed right after.

A woman pulled herself to her feet. She wore a long black dress that was covered in graveyard dirt. Her face was shaped like an oval, simple and pretty. She had wavy black hair down to her waist that she threw behind her shoulders in a mess of tendrils. Her hands and feet were black from clawing through the underworld.

When she looked at him, he knew. Beneath all that grime, Marius recognized her face.

His mother stood trembling. Her dark eyes looked around as if in a trance. She stared at the world like she was observing it instead of participating in it. A spectator watching the fish swim in an aquarium as opposed to swimming herself.

Marius limped up to her tentatively. This was partly because his ankle was killing him and partly because he wasn't sure it really was his mother. What if this was some terrible trick Rex was playing? He was a demon after all.

When he reached her, a gentle breeze wafted her scent his way. Sure, there was the grime and smell of fresh earth, but beneath that sat something familiar. The scent of the rosewood oil his mother brushed in her hair. Beneath that was the lilac laundry detergent she used on all their clothes. The faint whiff of freshly brewed coffee and sugar. Her smells.

"Marius," she said gently, gazing down at him.

Marius took in his mother's face with wide-eyed wonder. His mouth felt dry, and he realized it was hanging open. Her brown eyes squinted with her smile, creasing the laugh lines around the edges.

"Mom? Is it you?"

"Son, I think . . . I'm having the loveliest dream," his mother said.

When she spoke, it was with a tone of curious wonder, as if her mind did not believe her eyes. She turned this way and that, taking in their cemetery as though she had never seen it before.

"Am I dream walking? No, that can't be. They never let me dream. This can't be real."

"Mom, I think . . . I think this is real."

When she focused back on Marius, he saw the veil over her eyes lift. They became clearer in an instant, and she recognized him. Marius was barely able to breathe. He stood up awkwardly, favoring his broken ankle. His eyes scanned her all over as if trying to see if this was all true. Could she possibly be alive again?

Kelly Stone grabbed her son and wrapped him in an

embrace only a mother could do. The warmth of it, the feel of it, was known only to her and Marius. He sank inside himself and hugged her right back.

He had done it. He had brought her back. All the pain and suffering meant something. He had won after all. That terrible cold spot on his back finally warmed.

Marius lived in that triumphant moment. He breathed only in a world of his mother's embrace. In this place, he was safe. There were no monsters, no pain. The outside did not matter. So many muscles in his injured body relaxed. There would be no more lonely nights. No yearning for his mother. No more living as an outcast orphan boy.

His euphoria was only interrupted by the receding voice of Rex as he led the wendigo away, disappearing into the ether.

"She's all yours, baby hunter. You get what you pay for."

CHAPTER THIRTY-THREE

"Marius," Kelly said quietly. "I . . . I need to wash my face."

He loosened his embrace reluctantly, still holding on to her arms for support. The grime from her hands stained his jacket and skin, but he did not care. They made their way to the dock uneasily. His mother wobbled like she had not used her legs in some time.

At the edge of the dock, she pulled handfuls of bayou water to her face. It was not terribly clean, but it was better than nothing. After scrubbing her hands and face, she sat like a little girl, dangling her feet in the water. Marius sat next to her, afraid to say anything that might break the spell.

Kelly Stone's eyes lit up suddenly, and she turned to her son with renewed clarity.

"Marius. This is real? I'm really back?" she asked as though she still did not believe it.

"Yes, Mom. I brought you back," he said gently.

Her eyes grew even wider as though waves of under-standing kept crashing over her. She reached a wet hand across and grabbed his wrist.

"But how? How did you get the money?"

Marius looked down sheepishly at his oversized coat. He pulled his monster book from its pocket and laid it on the dock for the whole world to see. Conflicting emotions rattled in his gut. Pride with a touch of trepidation. When she looked back up at him, a rolling sense of guilt invited itself to the party.

His mother's expression changed again when she took him in. Finally, she was seeing him fully for the first time since she emerged from the ground. She placed one hand on his cheek and brushed his hair away from his eyes.

"You're older. So much older than you ought to be."

"It's been a while, Mom. You were gone a long time."

"How long? Where I was there was no telling time . . . ," she said, trailing off.

"Two years," he said softly. "You've been dead for two years."

Kelly sucked in a sharp breath. She whipped her head around, taking in the cemetery, the bayou, and her son. Her eyes pored over his ragged appearance and fell on his cast. She winced as though she felt the break herself.

"You've been all alone? All this time, you were here alone . . . monster hunting?"

Marius spotted the movement in the water. There was

the faintest shimmer of a set of scales and a wisp of hair. The pale creature moved through the bayou water soundlessly. Kelly Stone might have noticed if she was not so focused on Marius's face.

"Well, I wasn't totally alone."

He gestured to the water by her feet. The two watched as Rhiannon slowly emerged from the murky depths. His mother's eyes widened as she took in the teenage mermaid. Rhiannon rarely appeared nervous, but she did in that moment. Still, she did not break eye contact.

"Please don't freak out, Mom. Rhia is my friend. She helped me get you back."

Marius was not sure what he expected. After all, his mother had done her fair share of monster hunting in the past. A mermaid was a monster. Would she try to capture her? Hurt her? Tell others about her existence?

Much to his surprise, Kelly Stone relaxed her body and smiled at his friend. Rhiannon smiled back. It was such a satisfying sight. His two favorite people were meeting at last. Marius held his breath in anticipation of what might happen next.

"Oh, Marius, do you think I've never met a mermaid before?" she asked sweetly.

Marius's jaw dropped, and he struggled to regain his composure. His mother reached down and touched Rhiannon's cheek. The mermaid rested her face against her hand. There was such an ease to it. He wondered if maybe

Rhiannon needed what he needed. A mother to hold her. If she could not find her own mother, perhaps his would do.

"Thank you for watching after my boy." Kelly turned her attention back to Marius. "And I'm so sorry you were left alone. That should never have happened. I'm back now, son. You will never have to monster hunt again. You're safe. Both of you are safe."

When he thought about that, a tension in his body gave up the ghost. It wound between his ribs, across his chest, and around his heart. A terrible serpent of pain he never knew was there until it died.

As the snake tension withered away, Marius felt he could breathe again. His heart was free to beat the way it ought. He could be anything now. He could stop monster hunting if he wanted to. He could be a normal kid again. Well, normal for a cemetery boy.

His mother turned her attention back to Rhiannon, inspecting her shoulder. She muttered something about an herbal salve that would help them both heal. There was something about chewing lemon rinds for inflammation. He did not hear it all. Everything around him muted as he allowed wave after wave of relief to flood his soul.

Marius reached out and stroked the edge of his monster book. It hummed when his finger trailed the spine, almost like a cat purring when petted. He pulled it to his chest, holding it like an old friend. In that moment, he realized the book wasn't just a book. It had become a part of him. They drew blood together, fought together, dragged through the muck together. He could not just put it away.

A strange grin crossed his face as he thought about every monster he had captured. Every battle he had won against all odds. The smile grew when he thought about how many were still out there.

All those evil creatures to be defeated. All that Mystic money left to be collected.

Sure, he *could* stop monster hunting, he thought. His mother was back. His friends were safe. But the real question—the million dollar question—was, would he?

EPILOGUE

The monster hunter struggled to breathe. The crush restricted his movements from all sides. It felt like a python had wrapped itself around his body and was squeezing him to death. His lungs struggled to expand. At this rate, he would lose consciousness in minutes.

"You wicked child!" Mama Roux said as she finally released him. "How dare you run off after a rougarou like that. Losin' you would have been tha death of me."

Marius took in a deep gulp of air. Never had Mama Roux hugged him so hard and for so long. It was hard to tell if she was furious or worried. Maybe both.

"I'm sorry. I just had to," he said.

"Why? You tell me what foolhardy reason you had for a thing like dat?"

Anger colored her face, making her look like a stranger. Mama Roux was never angry.

"There was a spell I needed the money for."

"What spell?" she asked, setting her balled fists on her round hips.

Marius tried to think of a way to stall. What answer might pacify her?

He was not sure how she found out about the rougarou. The fringe community rumor mill could put a sewing circle to shame, but it took a whole week for the word to spread. The news was bound to get out. Luckily, no one seemed to know about the other part of the story yet.

It had been a week since his mother came back from Hell, and everyone was still in the dark about her return. She wanted it that way. A little peace to recover before everyone in the magical community bombarded them with questions.

One thing was clear. Someone had finally snitched about the monster, and since the only other people who knew about the rougarou were Madame Millet and Mildred, he had one guess who ratted him out.

"I can't tell you. Not right now," Marius said with the biggest hangdog expression he could muster. "What if I promise to explain it all soon?"

"How soon?"

"Real soon," he said, trying to make his eyes appear remorseful.

The monster hunter delivered the final blow. He closed the gap between them and hugged her around the waist. All the tension in Mama Roux's body relaxed, and she hugged him back. Not nearly as hard this time.

There was no better weapon to use against an angry mom.

"All right, child. Keep your secret for now. But I expect you to tell me soon," she said, releasing him once more. "I won't fulfill any more orders if you don't. Oh, look, here's your food now."

One of the cooks approached them with a large plastic bag. When he handed it to Marius, the smell overtook his senses. His stomach growled in anticipation. He wondered if the cook could hear it.

"Why have you been orderin' so much lately? I've hardly seen you or your ghosts all week. Just to-go orders," Mama Roux said. "Half the time you disappear before I can say a word to ya. Now I know why."

"Sorry about that. I've had company."

"What sort of company?"

"Thanks again for the food! Gotta go. Bye!"

Marius waved as he hurried out the door. The longer he stayed, the harder it would be to keep the secret.

Nightfall had not yet settled as he rounded the hill. There was still daylight to be enjoyed, but it was softening into those hazy oranges and purples of twilight. Everything slowed by degrees as the world eased into the moon stage. Marius breathed in the fresh air and breathed out any worries he felt.

The cemetery lay before him, and just beyond it, the dock. He limped toward it as the food bag bumped against his good leg. The tinkling of feminine laughter echoed across the bayou, and he smiled as he approached its source.

Kelly Stone sat cross-legged on the dock, her back against one of the support posts. Rhiannon's body was in the water, but she rested her elbows on the dock. A sincere smile spread across her face as she gazed up at his mother.

Marius grinned without realizing it. How long had it been since he smiled before this week? How long had it been since Rhiannon had?

Having a mother around changed the scenery. It felt like they did not have to try so hard anymore. There was someone there to make it better. Someone to make it stable. When you had that, the smiles came back.

"There he is!" Kelly said as she took in her son. "It's about time. What took you so long? We are starving."

"Rhia is always starving," Marius said with a chuckle.

"Well, this time, we are all starving," his mother said.

Marius joined them on the dock, plopping down on the wood and resting his back against the post across from his mother. Rhiannon floated in between them, staring at the bag with those intense eyes of hers.

"Mama Roux found out about the rougarou. She was not happy. There were a lot of hugs and questions," he said, eyeing his mother.

"She doesn't know about me, right?" Kelly asked.

"No, but I can't keep you hidden long. Eventually, people will find out you're back. It's a small community. Everybody talks."

"I promise this won't be much longer. Just need a little more time to adjust."

"I get that, but I'm sure Madame Millet will want to know. I'm surprised she hasn't invited herself over already to check in on me."

"I just need to make sure that everything's . . . okay. Nothing's wrong."

"What do you mean?"

Marius watched as her gaze drifted away. She stared out into the bayou as her eyes glazed over. It was like she had left the world for a moment.

"There is too much talking," Rhiannon said. Her words snapped Kelly out of her trance. "The food is right there. It's stupid not to eat it."

A dragonfly made the mistake of buzzing too close to the dock. Rhiannon's tongue whipped out and snatched it with ease. They heard a muffled crunch as she bit down.

Marius repressed a cringe and opened the bag. There were fried fish, gumbo, and hush puppies for him. His mother wanted étouffée and rice with cornbread. He'd ordered the largest portion of boiled crab he could, without Mama Roux asking too many questions, for Rhiannon. Plus, he had added two dozen boiled shrimp for everyone to share.

"Oh, this food. I swear there's no better étouffée in the world," his mother said through healthy bites.

Marius nodded as he peeled a shrimp and popped it into his mouth. The flavor lit up his tongue and cleared his sinuses.

"Did you get me anything?"

Everyone jumped as Hugo appeared suddenly next to them. The lutin gazed at Marius with hopeful eyes.

"You cannot eat," Rhiannon said.

"I know, but . . . I was hoping. . . . ," Hugo said, trailing off.

"Of course, I did," Marius said as he reached into the bag.

He pulled out a wax apple he had swiped before Mama Roux locked her arms around him. It looked realistic. Someone went through the trouble of placing tiny dots of hot glue along the top to simulate water droplets.

Hugo's eyes lit up as he took the apple.

"This is the best one! Everyone fights over this apple," he said.

"It's yours. You can keep it here and pretend anytime you like. Just don't tell the others or Mama Roux. She's cross with me as it is. She wouldn't be too happy if she knew I swiped one of her play apples," Marius said.

"I won't. Not a soul. Thank you!"

Hugo flew away, the shiny apple in his hands. After he

left, all eyes turned to the mermaid. Rhiannon was staring at her meal. She took one of the crabs from the box and looked at it dubiously.

"What's wrong?" Marius asked.

"Why is it this color?"

"It's cooked," Kelly said.

"And it has seasoning on it," Marius added.

"I like them better alive. They wiggle when you eat them," Rhiannon said.

The mermaid grimaced. It was an odd look on her, and Marius almost laughed. He was pretty sure she would be mad if he did that, so he pressed on.

"I think you'll like them cooked. It's spicy."

Rhiannon shrugged and opened her hideous maw. She dropped the whole crab in, shell and all. The crunch that followed was both sickening and amusing. It was much louder than the dragonfly, a series of pops and cracks. She swallowed after a few more seconds of chewing.

Marius and his mother watched her, waiting for a reaction. The whole thing was oddly fascinating. To their surprise, the mermaid nodded in approval.

"You like it?" Marius asked.

"I do not like that it does not wiggle, but the spicy part is good. Tastes like when you eat jellyfish and they sting your tongue."

"Here, you should try a shrimp," Marius said.

When he moved his arm to grab the shrimp box, his

oversized sleeve brushed over his bowl of gumbo. His mother reached across and grabbed his wrist. She turned it over and examined the wet stain on his jacket.

"Oh, Marius, I swear this thing gets dirtier every day. You have to take it off and let me wash it. You look like a ghoul."

"I . . . don't like taking it off."

"I know you don't, but I'm here now. No need to always be on alert."

The monster hunter hung his head. That thought had never occurred to him. Was that why he never took it off? Because he never felt safe enough to do so?

"Go on," his mother said with a wave of her hand. "Go take off that nasty thing and hang it by my washboard in the house. Off with you."

Marius grabbed a piece of fish and stuffed it into his mouth. He stood up with a groan and walked toward the family mausoleum. Once inside, he peeled off the coat and laid it over a nearby chair. There were a number of old stains. Bayou water, fish slime, and blood. Ones he had scrubbed over and over again, but never could get all the way clean.

"Ewww. She's right. It really does need a proper wash."

His stomach told him to hurry back to the dock. There was more food awaiting him. More warmth. More laughter. Marius had a hand on the door when a thought formed in the back of his brain. He stopped and turned back to his coat.

If his mother was going to wash his coat, he had better empty the pockets first. Sure, there were some pockets that were infinitely deep, but the last thing he wanted was to tempt fate and have something ruined. It took a long time to collect some of those ingredients.

Marius limped back over to his coat and began emptying the pockets. He lined the various flasks and vials on a nearby shelf. Holy water, brick dust, salt, and jasmine. Then there were the rosaries. Normal ones, blessed ones, and a new skull rosary he had picked up for Rhiannon. He planned to give that to her later.

The last thing was his monster book. Marius pulled it from the deepest pocket and held it as gently as if it were alive. There was a spot on the shelf next to a few other books that would be perfect. A safe place where it could blend in. Where people might not notice and go snooping.

The monster hunter looked around to check that he was alone. He opened the book to the latest page. There were no pictures on it. No description of a beast captured. Just a word written on the top. One that was a promise. An adventure waiting to happen.

Chupacabra

The name had arrived in the mail two days after his mother returned. A simple slip of paper with only a few sentences of information in an envelope with no return address. He didn't recognize the handwriting but added it to his book without thinking twice.

Marius shut the book quickly, using the mysterious envelope as a bookmark. He swiveled his head around one more time before sliding the book on the shelf. He left it there and headed back to the dock. Back to the food. Back to the laughter. Back to the family.

All would be normal again. The ghosts, the chores, and school were all waiting for him. But the book...well, that was his secret. His monster book would keep that secret for as long as it needed to.

ACKNOWLEDGMENTS

I would like to thank my mother for believing in me, supporting my creative endeavors since I was a kid, and telling me that being "normal" is boring. Mom, you could have freaked out when I was drawing hideous things in my playroom, but you didn't, and I love you for it.

A big thanks goes to my husband, Brian, who is my biggest fan and cheerleader. I wanted to give up so many times over the years. You believed in me when no one else did, including myself.

Thank you Ben Miller-Callihan and the staff at Handspun Literary. You are by far the best agent I've ever had and a sensational brainstorming partner.

Speaking of brainstorming partner, a huge thanks goes to my editor, Holly West, and the team at Feiwel and Friends. You took a chance on my little book, and I'm eternally grateful.

I want to thank the best beta readers an author could ask for, Janet Shawgo and Joan Acklin. You are the first people I send my books to, an amazing support system, and my dear friends.

Finally, I want to thank my Cajun family, who filled my life with laughter, stories, and the best food in the world. You love me even though I don't say "praline" correctly.

Thank you for reading this Feiwel & Friends book.
The friends who made BRICK DUST AND BONES possible are:

JEAN FEIWEL, Publisher
LIZ SZABLA, VP, Associate Publisher
RICH DEAS, Senior Creative Director
HOLLY WEST, Senior Editor
ANNA ROBERTO, Senior Editor
KAT BRZOZOWSKI, Senior Editor
DAWN RYAN, Executive Managing Editor
CELESTE CASS, Production Manager
EMILY SETTLE, Editor
RACHEL DIEBEL, Editor
FOYINSI ADEGBONMIRE, Associate Editor
BRITTANY GROVES, Assistant Editor
L. WHITT, Designer
HELEN SEACHRIST, Senior Production Editor

Follow us on Facebook or visit us online at mackids.com.
OUR BOOKS ARE FRIENDS FOR LIFE.